ROOF OVER OUR HEADS

*"I'll drive the buggy up Main Street," Vee said, "if you'll
be the girl."*

ROOF OVER OUR HEADS

By

MARGUERITE DICKSON

Illustrated by

JEAN MACDONALD PORTER

JUNIOR LITERARY GUILD
AND
THOMAS NELSON & SONS
Edinburgh NEW YORK Toronto

By the Same Author
LIGHTNING STRIKES TWICE
BRAMBLE BUSH

To

my son and my two daughters
who all love the Maine coast
as I do

CONTENTS

ILLUSTRATIONS

CHAPTER I

NO CHOICE

"Oh, Mums, I don't think I could bear it."

"I am not any more anxious to do it than you are, Georgia, but I really don't see anything else to do. We have the house there, and here we have nothing, nothing at all. Two weeks' pay coming to me, and no other job in sight."

Georgia looked steadily out of the window at the crowded, noisy street. "You always have been able to get a job when you needed one," she said, winking back the tears. "Why couldn't you now?"

Mrs. Lane straightened up after setting the dish of steaming potatoes on the small table. "I think you know why, Georgia," she said, "if you face the facts. The time when any woman could get a job is gone. We're lucky that I kept mine as long as I did. Now I haven't a chance."

She went to the little closet kitchenette and picked up the platter, in which were two small chops. "There could be worse things than going back to Lane's Cove," she said. "Come and eat your dinner while it is hot. We can't afford meat every night."

"It isn't any use to change the subject, Mums," said Georgia, seating herself at the table. "I'm not thinking about what we have to eat."

"Maybe you'd better think about it, daughter. Getting something to eat is one of the reasons—"

"Mums," Georgia interrupted in an exasperated burst, "you talk as if we might go hungry."

"Well, we might," said her mother soberly. "I have a little money saved, but it wouldn't last long here. Rent, plenty high for what we get," and she glanced around the small living room. Except for the kitchenette and bath, this was all they had. The bedroom was only an alcove off the living room.

"Rent," she repeated, "and food, harder to get and harder to pay for every day. Clothes, city clothes—"

"Don't we have to eat and have things to wear anywhere?" asked Georgia, in that hard-to-be-convinced tone she was apt to take when an argument wasn't going her way. "And rent," she added. "You pay your rent in taxes down there. It's just the same, isn't it?"

"Not quite. Twenty dollars a year tax for the house. Forty dollars a month for this—dump. Besides, we pay the taxes anyway. I own the house now."

"Mums! I never heard you talk like that before."

"Like what? Dump? That's what you call it. Why shouldn't I? Remember the time you wouldn't ask your Scout Patrol to meet here? You called it a hole in the wall that time."

"That was a joke," said Georgia. "What's for dessert?" She jumped up rather hastily, reaching for her mother's plate and picking up her own.

"I opened the last jar of Great-aunt Susan's plums," Mrs. Lane answered. "No more, until we put them up ourselves. The plum trees ought to be in bloom right now."

"You talk as if it was all settled, Mums. Usually you let me help you decide things."

"I'm afraid it is all settled. There isn't anything for anyone to decide. We can live there, we can't live here. It's as simple as that. At least we'll have a roof over our heads."

Georgia came back with the plums, gleaming red in their low glass dish, and set them down before her mother. "If that's the way it is," she said stiffly, "that's the way it is, I suppose. When does the exodus take place?"

Mrs. Lane laughed. "Don't be stuffy, darling," she said.

Before Georgia could answer, the doorbell, almost over their heads, rang a sharp tattoo, two short and one long. Georgia hurried to the button which released the door latch downstairs.

"Don't tell Lorraine yet, Mums," she said. "Maybe something will happen so we don't have to go. Maybe—maybe," rather grandly, "I'll get a job."

She had only time to catch her mother's derisive smile and shake of the head before Lorraine was at the door, bouncing in as always, in haste and full of excitement.

"Georgia," she shouted—Lorraine always shouted—"my dad says he'll let me go to camp. For all summer, maybe. Now you have to do it too. It would be twice the fun if you would."

And surprisingly enough, Georgia's answer to that was, "No can do, Lorrie. Mums and I are moving to the country, right away, I guess."

Georgia heard her mother say under her breath, "Unpredictable, absolutely." But she had no time even to think about what that meant. Lorraine had fallen upon her with: "The country? How perfectly marvelous! Where? Will you ask me to come and visit you? I'd lots rather do that than go to camp."

"Wait a minute, wait a minute!" Georgia held up her hands

as if to ward off the questions. "We haven't gone yet. We might not have a bed to put you in."

"There'll be beds, Lorraine," said Mrs. Lane. "And beds," she added. "Great-aunt Susan had a big family."

"Who was Great-aunt Susan?" Lorraine turned the attack on Mrs. Lane.

"It was her house," said Georgia. "She left it to Mums. It's an inheritance."

"Gosh!" said Lorraine. "Nobody ever left anything to anybody in our family. Pretty grand, I'd say. I'd love to live in the country."

"I wouldn't," said Georgia. "But what can you do when you inherit an estate? You have to go and keep it up."

"Georgia, Georgia!" said her mother. "It isn't that way at all, Lorraine. Great-aunt Susan did leave me the house, and there's land that goes with it. But it's far from anything I'd call an estate. And I probably wouldn't go to live there now, if I hadn't lost my job. I'm sure I wouldn't. I never meant to go back there again."

"Oh, poor Mrs. Lane," said Lorraine, with quick sympathy. "But maybe it's one of those ill winds that does blow some good. Pretty soon you'll probably be as glad as anything that you had to do it. Is it far away?"

"Quite far," said Mrs. Lane. "The coast of Maine. Country and ocean, woods and straggling villages. No summer resorts, no big towns. I lived there all my life until—lately. And Georgia was born there."

"In Great-aunt Susan's house?" asked Lorraine.

"No, in the Lane house in the village. Georgia's father was born there too."

"Who lives in that house now? Some other Lanes?"

"No, that house was sold. Georgia and I came to Boston after her father died. I had to earn our living."

"Tough luck," said Lorraine. "But if you hadn't come to Boston, I'd never have known Georgia, would I?"

Georgia had grown melancholy again. "You won't know me much longer," she said. "Pretty soon we'll just be gone."

"Stuff and nonsense," shouted Lorraine. "I'll always know you. And your mother says there are beds enough, so I'll come to visit you, the way I said. My dad says I ought to be put out to pasture, till I get over being such a noisy kid. Maybe you've got a pasture," and she laughed as she hooked her arm through Georgia's. "Come on," she said. "Let's walk down Cambridge Street and watch the sun set."

When Georgia came back to the apartment an hour later, she found her mother sitting at the little desk by the front window, with papers strewn before her and a frown of concentration between her eyes.

"I wish those Carminellos didn't make so much noise," she said absently. "You'd think there were forty children under the windows instead of half a dozen. Though you'd think I'd be used to it by this time."

There was no answer. Georgia had dropped disconsolately into a corner of the couch that became her bed at night.

"Lorrie doesn't know what she is talking about," she said after a while. " 'The country!' What is there in the country?"

"A roof over our heads," said her mother firmly. "I told you that before. And a roof's a valuable possession." She busied herself with the papers in front of her. "And beds!" she lifted her head to say a minute later. "*Not* in the living room, and not in a hole in the living room wall."

"You ought to have Lorrie for a daughter," said Georgia

bitterly. "She thinks the country's heaven. She could even make me think so for a minute or two, while she talked. But it isn't. I remember."

Her mother looked up abruptly. "How much do you remember?"

Her eyes were fixed steadily upon Georgia's.

"Oh, plenty," said Georgia carelessly. Her shoulders were slumped and her hands lay idle in her lap. "Even if I wasn't very old," she added.

"You were six," her mother said, almost sharply. "We've been here ten years. What do you remember?"

Georgia looked out through the window at the strip of darkening sky over the roofs across the street. "Mums," she said slowly, "what was there about Daddy, and the house, and our coming away? Was there something queer?"

"Is that why you don't want to go back?" Mrs. Lane rose from her chair and came over to stand in front of Georgia. "Tell me what it is that you remember."

Georgia struggled to her feet from the soft depths of the couch. "I don't really know," she said. "There was once in the post office, when I was waiting with Debbie for the mail. I heard an old man say something. I think I knew him then, but I don't know now who he was."

"What did he say?"

"He said to another man, 'That there's George Lane's kid.' And he looked fierce somehow. 'She an' her Ma's goin' to Boston. Live there in style, I make no doubt. Wonder how much of it the wife got.'"

Mrs. Lane sat down on the couch and drew Georgia down beside her. "I guess you can't run away from things, daughter," she said. "Sometimes I wish I hadn't tried."

Georgia's eyes opened wide. "Were we running away when we came to Boston?"

"Was I, you mean. I would have said no when I did it. I had our living to earn. But I was glad to go away. I thought we'd never go back."

"What was it, Mums?" The eyes were terrified now. "What was it?"

"Don't look like that, child. It was about money. There was an accident. Your father's car went off the bridge in an icy skid, and he was killed. And the same day they found a lot of money missing from the bank. His accounts seemed to be all right, but some money that should have been in the safe just wasn't there. So they thought that he had taken it."

"Just like that," said Georgia scornfully. "Why did they think so? Did they find the money?"

"No, they never found it. And that's really the whole story. They never found out anything about it at all, and they never tried to prove that he took it. There was no evidence against him. But a good many people thought they didn't need proof. He was the cashier, and the money was gone."

Georgia was quiet now, piecing together what she had just heard with what she remembered. "That's what the man meant," she said. "He thought you had the money."

"I suppose so," said her mother. "He wasn't the only one. Mostly they were the people who didn't much believe in banks, anyway. Losing their money seemed the worst thing that could happen to them, so they forgot friendship and trust, and even Christian charity. The old ones were the worst, the kind who thought an old stocking was the best bank."

"So we ran away, and let them think you had it."

"Not exactly. That was why I sold the house. It was a fine

house, for a place like Lane's Cove, and it brought enough, with what other money I could raise, to cover the loss."

"Oh, Mums, you didn't? That was like saying you knew he took it."

"No. They knew what I thought. At first the bank directors refused it, and then said it should be merely a loan. And I said: 'Very well. When you've found out who did take the money, and can clear my husband's name, I'll take this back.' And we took the train for Boston."

By this time the street outside was quiet, and for a moment there was no sound inside the room. Then Georgia threw herself down with her head in her mother's lap.

"I can't go back," she said, her face buried, her voice muffled and broken. "And you mustn't either. Everybody would look at us—"

Her mother lifted her up briskly, and handed her a handkerchief. "Don't be silly, daughter," she said. "Everybody'll look at us anyhow. A stranger in Lane's Cove merits that much attention, even a stranger who really isn't a stranger at all. Perhaps that kind more than any other. Don't go imagining things. I have plenty of friends in Lane's Cove, friends who know that George Lane didn't do crooked things. Probably the whole story's been forgotten long ago, anyway. We'll just be 'the Lanes,' come home from Boston."

Georgia had stopped crying as suddenly as she had begun. "The Lanes?" she said. "Are we the only ones left?"

"The only ones likely to come back to Lane's Cove. It's queer how the old families die out, or disappear from their home towns."

"Have the Burnhams died out too?"

"Just the same. There were Lanes or Burnhams in half the

houses in town when I was your age. My mother had twenty-one cousins on the Burnham side, and I don't know how many on the other, because that side came from 'away,' as they used to say. And now that Great-aunt Susan is gone, there isn't a Burnham left in the town. Or a Lane either, till we get back."

She went to the desk. "I've been making lists of what to take, and what to sell off to the secondhand men. There really isn't much here. Holes-in-the-wall don't have room for much. And we'll find the house at the Point furnished, even if everything isn't exactly as we would choose. There! I've talked long enough. Getting to be a regular chatterbox."

And with determined cheerfulness she set about preparations for bed.

Georgia went slowly about the business of taking off the cushions from the couch, folding down the couch cover, getting her bed pillows from the chest under the window, and pulling the couch from the wall so that the blankets would be free and comfortable when she should be under them.

When her mother came out from the tiny bathroom, Georgia was ready to go in, but the business of washing, and brushing her teeth, was even more mechanical than usual as she turned over in her mind the changes ahead of her.

"I shall hate everything about it," she thought, knowing now that she must submit without further protest.

Absorbed in contemplation of the various things she would hate, she was unconscious for the moment of what she would be giving up. Then suddenly that came rushing upon her. The school where all her friends were, and where she would be a senior next year; Glee Club practice on Monday nights; the branch library up Cambridge Street, housed in the old West Church of colonial days, to which she could go so easily and so often; her Scout troop; Saturday morning art class at the Museum; and Lorraine. Lorraine most of all.

"A roof over our heads!"

It couldn't be worth all she was giving up. Tossing her towel furiously at the rack, she dashed out of the bathroom, and without a word of good night to her mother lunged across the room to her bed.

"A roof over our heads! A roof over our heads!"

The monotonous refrain repeated itself over and over till, fighting to the last against all that it stood for, she went to sleep.

CHAPTER 2

FAREWELLS

The next two weeks were full of confusion and excitement for Georgia. "Shall we keep it or let it go to the secondhand shop?" was the question to be met about something every day. There was the sad matter of closing up her school affairs, with a farewell party given for her at the home of one of the girls. There was the last meeting with the Glee Club, and the last Saturday morning art class. And there were long hours with Lorraine, in which they discussed the future of their friendship.

"Of course I won't forget you," said Lorraine with scarcely concealed impatience. "You always find such a black side to look at."

They were walking on the Esplanade, green with freshly cut grass, and bright with the water of the River Basin glittering in the sun.

"This is a lovely place," said Georgia, turning the subject neatly. "What do I want of the country?"

"It isn't what you want," said Lorraine practically, "but what you're going to get. So you'd better like it. Anyway, won't you be glad to get away from Kendall Street, with its sooty chimneys and the everlasting noise of those Carminello kids?"

"Our block isn't so bad," said Georgia, quick to defend the blessings that were taking their flight. "Over toward the other end the street is pretty awful. But I've lived on Kendall Street a long time."

"So have I," said Lorraine. "It won't be the same with you gone." She looked off to the Basin, where a saucy little speed boat was scooting off up the river. "I remember when you first came. Weren't you the scared little kid?" Her momentary gloom seemed to be quite dispelled, with the grin she turned on Georgia.

"I remember, too," said Georgia. "The Carminellos—I mean Tony and Luigi, and their gang that's all grown-up now—they used to scare me to death with their cops-and-robbers game, and the way they used to yell at each other. I'd never heard anything like that."

"Do you remember Lane's Cove?" asked Lorraine.

"Some," said Georgia. "I remember the lilacs, big old bushes almost like trees. They used to smell wonderful in the spring."

"There, see!" said Lorraine. "You like the country, all right, only you just don't know it. What else do you remember?"

Georgia laughed. "I remember my kitten, all white, with beautiful blue eyes. She was the craziest thing, climbing over everything, roughing up her back if even a leaf blew her way, and chasing her tail till it made me dizzy to watch her."

"What became of her? You didn't bring her with you."

"I think Mums gave her to Great-aunt Susan. I'm sure she did."

"Maybe you'll find her there, sitting on the doorstep waiting for you. But she wouldn't be a kitten now."

"Well, I'm not a kitten either."

"Do you remember the Lane house, and Great-aunt Susan's?"

"The Lane house, a little. I never lived in Great-aunt Susan's house. I don't even know very well where it is, except that it's out of the village. Mums wouldn't ever talk to me about Lane's Cove, anyway. She'd just say, 'Oh, we left all that years ago. It doesn't matter.' Or, 'There's nothing of ours left there.' And then change the subject."

Lorraine caught sight of the clock high above the Basin on the Cambridge side.

"Gosh!" she said. "That says five o'clock. I'll have to hop, skip and jump to get home, so I can peel the beloved potatoes. Sometimes I wish there weren't quite so many people in my house to peel for. You have it easy with only two."

But Georgia's mind was still on Lane's Cove as they walked back to Kendall Street. Debbie, the big girl next door, had been with her that day at the post office. Had she thought the same things about Daddy that the old man had thought? Did Debbie still live next door to the Lane house? Georgia hoped she didn't. She wished that there would be no one left who remembered that old troubled time. And she wished most of all that she, herself, did not have to face Lane's Cove. But it was no use to wish. She shrugged off her thoughts, and began to listen again to Lorraine's chatter.

One by one the days went by. The little apartment grew bare as curtains, pictures and china went into boxes and cartons. Mums stopped working, and spent all day packing, or in settling up the final bills. Georgia took back her books to the library for the last time, and went shopping with Mums.

Lorraine brought her a parting gift, stationery, "so you'll be sure to write," she said.

At the last Georgia was surprised to find how kind the noisy, careless neighborhood could be. Mrs. Carminello, with the newest baby in her arms and a trail of near-babies behind her, came with ravioli for their dinner that last night. Miss Asher, the old doctor's almost as old housekeeper, brought a jar of the doctor's "brown salve," famous in the neighborhood for healing all the cuts, burns and bruises that such a lively neighborhood was always suffering. The Roche boys, with bold, admiring looks at Georgia, offered their latest comic books to be read on the train. Mrs. Pulaski, next door, came to say: "Breakfast coffee at eight, in my kitchen. Or will that not be early enough? Then come when you will." And, with her flashing dark smile, she was gone before they could say anything at all to her.

But the most astonishing thing was the note from Mrs. Allerton. Almost no one on the street ever saw Mrs. Allerton. Her house, directly across the street, was one of the really old ones. One of a row of three, built of brick with a bow front and floor-length windows circled by a narrow balcony with a fanciful wrought iron railing in front, it had been elegant in its day, and even now kept much of its ancient dignity. Four stories of dignity, inhabited by one woman, alone. Everybody wondered what was inside, and wished Mrs. Allerton would ask someone from the street in just once, so that all could know. And now came the note.

"How did she know we are going away?" Georgia asked, with a puzzled frown.

"She must know more about us than we do about her, that is sure," her mother answered. "She says, 'It will be difficult to arrange for that last night, perhaps. There are beds in my house, and I am airing the sheets to make them ready for you. Ring the bell twice when you come. You will be welcome.'"

"Isn't it exciting, Mums?"

"It is very kind. I think it must be hard for her to open her door after all this time. They are all kind."

"Aren't they?" said Georgia, wonderingly. "Some of them I hardly know. And they are such funny people."

"They seem so because they are different from us. They probably think we're funny, too. Now pack your bag, daughter, and then we'll look around to make sure that all the last things are done. I'll write a little note to Mrs. Allerton and you can tuck it in her mailbox. What have I done with my pen?"

The apartment looked cold and unfriendly, with nothing left but the bare bed, the couch, also stripped to its mattress, and a few other pieces of furniture that the secondhand man would come for tomorrow. Georgia could not think of it as home any longer. Nor could she look forward to Great-aunt Susan's house as home either. She felt detached, with no roots anywhere.

Lorraine's familiar two short and one long on the bell cut into Georgia's thoughts sharply.

"What do you think?" Lorraine began when she had burst into the room. "The old lady—"

"You mean Mrs. Allerton?" said Mrs. Lane.

"Yes, Mrs. Allerton," Lorraine amended, looking slightly abashed. "She called up. I didn't even know she had a phone."

"Well, you wouldn't know that, unless you looked in the book to see," said Georgia. "What did she call up for?"

"You could have knocked me over with a feather," said Lorraine. "Why didn't you tell me you were going to sleep there? There, in that house!" She rolled her eyes and threw up her hands, apparently to express her great excitement.

"But what did she want of you?" Georgia was getting impatient.

"She said," and Lorraine paused impressively, " 'I have asked your friend Georgia and her mother to spend the night with me.' I almost dropped the phone at that, but I gasped out something. And she said—" Another pause.

"Go on!" threatened Georgia, "or I'll shake it out of you."

"She said," Lorraine repeated, " 'Would you like to come also, to spend this last night with your friend?' "

"What?" said Georgia. "Oh, that's perfect. You can see the house!"

"Exactly what I thought. It will be fun to see it together. What do you suppose it's like?"

"What I am thinking about," said Mrs. Lane, "is Mrs. Allerton, much more than the house. She knows about us all, it seems. I think she must sit all day behind those closed white curtains, getting acquainted with us."

"Kind of one-sided acquaintance," said Georgia.

"Well, now for some reason she wants to make it two-sided. So be sure you do your share. Don't think only of the house. Here, take my note and slip over quietly with it to the mailbox."

"All right, Mums. We'll think about her. But we want to see the inside of the house, just the same."

After they had eaten Mrs. Carminello's ravioli, and had rinsed the dishes under the faucet, Georgia ran over to return them, leaving her mother to set the bags outside in the hall and and to close the door for the last time. It was about half-past eight when Georgia and Lorraine came back together, and they all crossed the street.

"I'm so excited!" whispered Georgia while they were waiting for their double ring to be answered. "I think I shall burst!"

"Don't do that, dopey," said Lorraine. "Then you'd miss everything." She suppressed a giggle as the door opened.

Mrs. Allerton surprised them, calmly sweeping aside the strangeness of the situation, receiving them as if they were already acquaintances. "I have seen you often," she said to Mrs. Lane, "and when I heard that you were going away—"

"How did you know they were going?" asked Lorraine bluntly.

"You hear a great deal in a noisy neighborhood like this one," Mrs. Allerton answered. "Whether you wish to hear, or not," she added.

There had been some conversation after that while they sat for a few minutes before Mrs. Allerton showed them to their rooms.

"If you are leaving early, you will want a long night," she said, leading the way up the long wide stairway, softly carpeted and giving back no sound as they went up.

"I have put you two girls together," she said, opening a door near the head of the stairs. "I thought you would like that. And Mrs. Lane will be near you, in the next room down the hall. Good night."

She stepped back, closing the door, and Georgia could hear the voices of the two women in that next room. Then there was another good night and the sound of another door closing. After that everything was quiet and there was nothing to do but get ready for bed.

"We didn't say good night to Mums," said Georgia as she opened her bag to take out the necessities for the night. "Let's slip in now before any of us gets undressed. I feel as if none of this was real. Sort of fairy castle sort of thing." The two tiptoed down the hall to Mrs. Lane's door.

Later, they settled themselves in the huge bed with a black walnut headboard that seemed reaching for the ceiling. All the rest of the furniture in the room was of the same dark wood and, it seemed to the girls, of mammoth size.

"This wouldn't fit into one of our apartment bedrooms," said Lorraine.

"I should say not," answered Georgia. "You couldn't even get it into our apartment at all." She wished they could see more of this house. There were so many other rooms besides those they had seen.

The "drawing room"—she really called it that, "like in a book," Lorraine recalled now when they began to talk about it—was "faded, but elegant," Georgia said. There were heavy old brocade draperies and filmy lace at the windows; a long low sofa with grape carving at the top of the frame and with a multitude of buttons studding the upholstered back; soft heavy carpet under their feet, and a crystal chandelier over their heads, its pendants swinging in the draft from the open door.

"Nothing else like that on Kendall Street," said Lorraine now, "nor like the hall and stairs either. What did you think of the fancy bronze lady that stood on the newel post and held the light up in one hand?" She sat up in bed, thrusting one arm high to demonstrate. "Regular Statue of Liberty, huh?"

"Suppose all the houses on the street were like that, once?" was Georgia's only answer. "It's like pictures they show us in the interior decorating class. I'd like to stay here a week and look at everything."

"What did you think of her?"

"Mrs. Allerton?" Georgia paused to shift her mind from the house to its owner. "I don't know what I thought she'd be

"It's funny the way Mrs. Allerton stays shut in here,"
Lorraine said.

like," she said slowly, "but whatever it was, she isn't like it. Why, she isn't even awfully old, the way I expected."

"No, she isn't," agreed Lorraine. "Funny, the way she stays shut in here." Then she seemed to have a sudden idea. She sat up again. "Bet it's because she didn't like what the street got to be, nor the people that moved here. Noisy, the Carminellos; dirty, those awful Minichiellos that sit out on the sidewalk all summer. They don't give tone to any neighborhood." She flopped down again in the bed, smothering her giggles under the bedclothes, fine old linens and faded down quilt, light as air.

"That might be it," Georgia said slowly. "Those cheap rooming houses, too, on either side of her in what were 'residences' once, fine like hers. I can see how she would feel."

Mrs. Allerton had been the perfect hostess, formal, gracious, not even dressed queerly as the girls had anticipated.

"I thought she'd be like old pictures you see," Georgia said now. "Long funny skirts, maybe flowing sleeves and a kerchief at the neck. But she looks just like other people. I wonder if she does stay in this house all the time, the way they say she does."

"There's a garden at the back," Lorraine contributed. "You can see it from the Najarians' around on Watson Street. It has one huge tree in it, and bushes, maybe lilacs. I wouldn't know. There are flowers, too, in summer. She could walk round and round the garden path for her exercise. Or maybe she goes out that way, so Kendall Street won't see her. She's a stubborn piece, anyhow. She's got an idea, and she sticks to it, whatever it is."

"Wonder what she'd think if she knew the Carminellos brought us our dinner, and that we'll have breakfast in the

Pulaskis' kitchen." It was Georgia who giggled this time. "I still don't understand why she asked us."

"If you weren't going away, we could be nice to her, in return," said Lorraine.

"You're not going away. You can be nice to her, without me."

"If she'll let me. I'm not sure she would. Anyway, I might try, and when I come to see you, I'll tell you all about it."

"You'll really come, won't you, Lorrie? It's one of the things that helps me bear up. You don't know how I dread it all."

"Why? Why?" said Lorraine. "It's a new experience. You don't want always to do the same thing, do you?"

Georgia had a fleeting thought of telling Lorraine about the bank and the money and what people thought and how they would look at "the Lanes, come home from Boston." But she said nothing except: "I don't know how to live in the country. I'm a city girl. I like to live the city way."

"You wait and see," cheerfully. "Bet you'll adore it before you've been there six months. I would, I know that."

"Bet I won't. A thousand times I'll want to come back. Kendall Street is noisy and sooty and we had to live here all in a heap in not much more than one room, but I'll want to come back."

The next morning there was breakfast in Mrs. Pulaski's bright warm kitchen, then the unusual luxury of a taxi for the short ride to North Station.

"We could walk, I know," said Mrs. Lane, "but there are the bags."

So Tony Carminello, grown up to be a taxi driver, stopped the cab before Mrs. Pulaski's door with a flourish, and the whole neighborhood came out to say good-by. There was even the wave of a hand from between the curtains at the Allerton house.

Georgia had hard work to keep from spoiling the occasion with tears, but she succeeded in holding them back, and Tony started the car, with a shout of "Out of the road, kids!"

In a moment they had left Kendall Street, had swung around the corner into Green, then Leverett, and were headed straight for North Station. And what? Georgia wished she knew.

CHAPTER 3

HACKMATACK POINT

Once in the train, it seemed to Georgia that she had left her whole life behind, and she looked out of the window dolefully. She wondered how Mums could be so cheerful, until she remembered that, no matter what people in Lane's Cove might say or think, it was home to which Mums was going.

"I haven't any home now," she thought, in a sort of desperation of misery. "I don't belong anywhere." And she hugged the thought to her, establishing her grievance in her own mind, at least.

After Portland, the train was no longer express, but stopped at the more important places—Brunswick, Augusta, Waterville. Georgia roused enough after a while to reach for the timetable and study the map inside.

It was midafternoon when they pulled out from Bangor, where they had changed to another train. This was a short train, locomotive old style, cars shabby, roadbed bumpy, and, surprisingly, only one track. Georgia discovered that when on a long curve she could see the track ahead of the train.

The whistle blew every few minutes, with a long mournful but musical sound, as the train approached, stopped at, and then left behind the little gray-painted stations which all looked alike. At the stations an automobile or two would be waiting, a few scattered people standing about. Some of the stations seemed to sit quite alone, with nothing near to show the villages they served.

"Where are the houses?" Georgia asked once.

"Just down the road a piece," Mrs. Lane answered somewhat absently.

"Down the road a piece," Georgia echoed with disapproval. "Are you going to begin talking as if you'd always lived in the country?"

"Well, I have, except these last ten years. Don't start in feeling superior, daughter. If the people here could see our place in Kendall Street, they would feel sorry for us, and maybe in their hearts a little superior. But I hope they wouldn't show it, and you certainly must not. Give Lane's Cove a chance. You are condemning it before you even get there."

Georgia made no answer, turning all her attention on the view from the train window. Sharp-pointed evergreens cut the sky above the rounded tops of maple and birch; blue hills, some of them high enough to be called mountains, showed here and there where the trees were not too close and thick; sometimes, and often suddenly, they would come upon a little lake, clear and blue against the green.

She reached for the map again, and pored over it as the train chugged along from one little village to another.

"We go back to the edge, don't we?" she said after a while.

"The edge? Oh, you mean the shore."

"Yes. Lane's Cove's on it, I guess."

"It certainly is. When I was a little girl, they built ships in the Lane's Cove yards, big ships, too. But the yards have been closed for years. Steamships took the place of sailing vessels, and steel took the place of wood."

But Georgia was not more than half listening. Three stations more and they would reach Lane's Cove. She hoped nobody knew they were coming. It would be so much easier to slip into town quietly and then bury themselves in Great-aunt Susan's house before people could begin to stare.

The whistle blew almost constantly now. The villages were only a few miles apart. One station, two stations, then the conductor was saying, "Lane's Cove, Lane's Cove!" and a minute later was helping them down to the platform with the bags.

Georgia looked around apprehensively. But the platform was almost deserted, and without the wail of the train whistle the stillness struck her like a blow. Then it was broken by the thud of mailbags tossed out from the mail car and picked up deftly from the platform by a man in overalls, and by the bang of trunks and boxes from the express car.

The conductor did not bother to shout, "A-all a-bo-ard!" as he had done at most of the other stations. There was no one to get aboard. In no time at all, the train swung slowly into motion and disappeared up the track, around a curve, and out of sight.

The station master lifted and shoved the trunks and boxes, the little mail truck rattled off down the road.

"Aren't there any taxis?" asked Georgia.

"We're being met," her mother answered. "It's all arranged, but Vee seems to be late."

"I'll say he does," said Georgia. "Who is Vee? Why don't I know about these things?"

Before her mother could answer, a car came hurrying around

the corner into the short station road, seemed certain to collide with the mail truck, swerved out around it and came to a noisy stop in front of them.

The car door opened, a red-haired boy in dungarees leaped out, and the door shut with a bang, all in a second, Georgia thought.

"Gee, I'm sorry not to get here on time," said the boy. "That's the way. Be here, and the train's half an hour late. But be late, and gosh, it's right on the dot. Ma said you'd think nobody was meeting you at all if I was late. Hope you weren't thinking that."

"Now, who is he?" Georgia was thinking while her mother answered the boy. "Mums must have asked him, or somebody, to come. And she never told me."

She acknowledged her mother's brief introduction stiffly, but the boy showed no concern or embarrassment. His name, Vincent Allen, struck an answering chord somewhere in Georgia's early memories, but the remembrance was elusive and she had no time to tie it down to fact.

"Nobody ever calls me Vincent," the boy said, looking directly at Georgia. "There's one of us in every generation. Always Vincent Lockwood Allen. Some mouthful! But they don't ever get called that. My dad's Vince. I'm just Vee. I wouldn't know how to answer to anything but that."

He grinned companionably, seized the bags and opened the back door of the dusty car. When Mrs. Lane was seated, Vee turned to Georgia.

"How about sitting in front with me?" he asked with another of those wide grins, and before she had time to say either yes or no, there she was, already seated, and he was on the driving side, pressing the starter.

"You're named for your dad, same as I am for mine," he began the conversation. "I remember him, George Lane, I mean."

Georgia stiffened. Now it was coming. He remembered, and he did not lose any time in saying so. She made no answer, but looked straight ahead.

They were in what was probably the main street of the village, with a few stores, a church with a tall white steeple, the post office with "Lane's Cove" over the door. Then the car turned sharply to the right, into another street which soon turned frankly into a country road.

Georgia searched her mind for memories of Main Street, but found none. And the country road could have been anywhere. The boy went on talking, but luckily more over his shoulder to Mums than to her. They both seemed perfectly cheerful and neither seemed to mind that Georgia had nothing to say.

Once she did break into a momentary silence to ask, "How far is it, Mums?" but it was Vee who answered promptly: "Four and a half, to my house, that is. You're about a quarter farther on."

He was a neighbor! She would have to see him whether she wanted to or not. See him, listen to his chatter, and be always on the watch for the next reference to what he remembered about her father.

"Too bad I didn't get to see the train," he was saying now. "Wanted to know whether they're still using that old type locomotive. They'll have to be hauling longer trains soon as the summer season starts, and they'll have to put on some decent equipment. This stretch of road has the poorest service in the whole of eastern Maine."

Georgia had no intention of entering the conversation, but

quite to her own astonishment she said at this point: "What do you care? I don't believe you travel on it much."

"No," said Vee, with another of those good-natured grins. Georgia saw this one before she hastily turned her head, to look out of the side window. But he went on, just as if he thought she really wanted to know. "I'd like to, a lot more than I do, but there's plenty you can find out about railroads without going on them. I know a lot about equipment, I've got a wonderful collection of timetables, and I plan trips to all kinds of places—"

"Timetables!" scoffed Georgia. "And trips, on paper. What does that get you?" She seemed impelled to talk back, though what she meant to do was ignore him. She shut her lips tightly.

"It gets me fun," said Vee. "That's what I do it for." He took his right hand off the wheel and pointed at the road ahead. "We're coming to the Corners," he said, "and we're going to turn left there in front of the schoolhouse, onto the Hackmatack Point road. See?" and he swung the car by the freshly painted white schoolhouse, off the tar road and onto gravel.

"What's Hackmatack Point? For that matter, what's hackmatack?"

Vee looked astonished. "Hackmatack's a tree. See those over there, the tall slender feathery ones, with the sharpest points of all? A summer boarder we had once called them tamarack, and she said some folks say larch. But down here they're hackmatack." He spoke positively. "And where you're going to live is Hackmatack Point because the whole point's about covered with them, with a sprinkling of white birch," he conceded. "It's a sightly place. I've lived there all my life."

Loose gravel crunched under the car, but they rolled along comfortably enough. For a minute or two the road ran through light woods, then passed a short road leading to a cleared place where a house sat on a knoll.

"The Fairchilds'," said Vee. "Mona Fairchild's about your age. Nice girl."

More woods, then open fields.

"Now we're coming to our place," he said, with obvious pride. And it was a good-looking place, Georgia had to admit, trimly painted, fields neatly fenced, everything looking cared for. "All right, huh?" was Vee's comment.

For the first time, Georgia turned and really looked at him. "You *like* it, don't you?" she said. "Even out here, away from everything."

"Don't be a dope," said Vee flatly. "Yeah, I like it." His bright blue eyes snapped wide open, and he looked a little belligerent as he turned his head to face Georgia. "We've got things the city never dreamed of. Bet you lived there like a couple of rabbits in a burrow, but we've got *room*. That's what I like, room!"

His belligerence died promptly, even before Georgia said, with an air of being vastly entertained: "Well, you needn't snap my head off. We don't have to like the same things. Me for the rabbit burrow."

The road crossed a tiny brook, the car rattling over the three-plank bridge. Hackmatack Point! So this was where Great-aunt Susan's house was.

"Isn't there water?" she asked.

"Of course there's water," Vee answered. "Don't you know *anything* about it?"

"No," said Georgia carelessly. "I haven't much wanted to know." Then coldly, "I told you, I don't like the country."

Vee showed no trace of belligerence this time. "Isn't that a little narrow-minded?" he said judicially. "Did you ever live in the country? But of course you did. You lived in Lane's Cove until—"

Georgia hastened to fill that gap. "Until I was six. Until my father died." And then defiantly, "Until—"

"Georgia," said her mother quietly. There was a definite silence. Then Mrs. Lane went on, "We're almost there. Look, there's the roof just showing between the trees."

A roof over our heads! A roof over our heads! The refrain began to sing itself over and over in Georgia's mind, as it had done that night in Kendall Street when Mums had said: "We can live there. We can't live here. It's as simple as that. We shall at least have a roof over our heads."

The house was in plain sight now. Facing the east, it was low, gray, shadowed by a huge maple with a double trunk. "Not a hackmatack, thank goodness," Georgia thought. She had a distinct prejudice against hackmatacks already.

The big maple spread widely, its boughs extending from the edge of the low roof almost to the road, fifty feet away. In front of it the late afternoon shadows made a pattern across the road, and toward the south was a broad meadow, still bright with the last rays from the setting sun. To the left of the road a thin grove of slender white birches, and back of them a wide stretch of water.

"Arrowhead Bay," explained Vee. "You see there is water."

Was he being sarcastic? Georgia looked at him but could not decide. She looked back from the water to the house.

"Unpainted," she said scornfully, to herself. "Just gray. Just a tumble-down old house, and a tree. What a place to live!"

Then she caught a glimpse of a big bush, not far from the tree. A big bush, with gnarled old boughs. Lilacs! It was too early for blossoms, but she drew in her breath, as if she were really smelling the fragrance she remembered. It was wonderful, as she had told Lorraine.

The car had passed the house, turned into a short driveway and stopped. Vee was quick to help them out and in a moment they were walking toward the nearest door. "Leave the bags," he said. "I'll bring them in."

This must be the kitchen door, Georgia thought. The front door would be the one with sidelights, over beyond the lilacs. This door was open, and surprisingly, a woman stood in the doorway, smiling at them. From behind her came a smell of something cooking, and this time Georgia knew she was hungry. Didn't it smell good?

The woman was out on the doorstep now, with outstretched arms.

"Susie," she said. "Susie! It's so good to see you. Why did you ever stay away so long?" And Mums was inside those widespread arms, laughing and half crying.

"I don't know, Mart," she said. "I think now I should have come back long ago. But I'm here now."

Georgia felt a little left out of this reunion, but Vee was doing what he could. "That's Ma," he said. "They used to be buddies. Well, not exactly," he amended, "but whatever girls are, like that. They'll remember you in a minute. And see! Here's something we brought you." He pointed toward the door. "Guess she's had her supper. She's washing up."

Georgia followed his pointing finger with her eyes. "Oh, no," she gasped. "Not really? Pom! Pom!" And she was down on her knees before the open door, reaching for the white cat who sat there sedately washing her face. White, with blue eyes. Sky blue, just as she had told Lorraine. Sky blue! Beautiful!

CHAPTER 4

QUICK TOUR

"Of course you'll stay and eat with us, Mart. Both of you," and Mrs. Lane looked over to where Vee was watching Georgia smooth Pom's white head. They were all in the kitchen now, and Georgia wondered what it was that smelled so good in the covered pan on the stove.

"No, we won't stay. We had ours before Vee brought me down. We eat early. I just want a look at Georgia—little George, we used to call her, remember?—and then Vee and I will run along. It's your home now, and I think you should have it to yourselves for your first meal. Isn't it funny that we should both come to Hackmatack and live almost as near each other as when we were girls in the village?"

"Something much better than funny for me," said Mrs. Lane. "Georgia, come and meet your Aunt Martha."

Georgia put Pom down and came forward. She looked a little puzzled. "Mums," she said, "I thought you said there weren't any Lanes or any Burnhams here now. How do I get an aunt?"

"Not really an aunt," said Mrs. Allen, "but you always called me that. 'Auntie Martie,' you used to say. Now you are so tall and grown-up, your mother is promoting you to 'Aunt Martha.' We must be dignified."

She gave an exaggerated pat to her ruffled reddish hair, smiling that same wide smile Vee had. The hair was like his, too, but Georgia hoped she didn't air her views at the drop of a hat, the way he did. Nor talk about railroads as if they were interesting. Railroads! Aunt Martha looked pleasant. Perhaps it would be nice to have an aunt.

Then they were all outdoors again and walking toward the car.

"That makes me some kind of cousin," said Vee as he and Georgia followed the two mothers.

"Does it?" answered Georgia coolly. "Thanks for the buggy ride."

"Oh, there'll be a lot of those. You not having a car, you know. Women are always having to go to town for something or other."

"But surely we needn't trouble you with our something or others," Georgia said with a hint of sarcasm in her courtesy. "We have to learn to be miles away from everything, and to get along without, and like it."

"Suit yourself, if you want to be a martyr. But I bet Susie won't be like that."

Susie! Did he mean her mother? Fresh kid! "Do you—" she began indignantly.

"Sure I mean Susie. I don't have to say 'Mums,' do I? Or do I?"

"You don't have to say anything at all. You don't even have to think anything at all, about us. We'll do very well by ourselves."

She stood still, leaving him to go on alone to the car. But

he didn't seem to mind that. In two of his long leaps he was there. Now he had started the engine and was backing out of the driveway, with a last grin and a tantalizing wave of his hand.

"Country boys have no manners," she announced as her mother joined her for the few steps back to the house.

"How about city girls? You must try to get along with Vee. They're our nearest neighbors, and Mart's my best friend in Lane's Cove. I think Vee's rather nice."

"I like his mother," Georgia conceded. "Now let's look at the place. Funny little dump."

"Another dump? I thought we'd left that behind." Mrs. Lane looked troubled, as she stepped inside and held the screen door open for Georgia. "Are you going to be difficult every step of the way, daughter? From now on, this is our home, the home I am providing for you. You might pay me the courtesy of appreciating that fact."

"Mums, Mums, I didn't mean anything. Dump's just a word, just a place, any place." She looked around her at the plain but spotless kitchen, and then back at her mother, who still stood without a smile.

"It is—different, Mumsie. You'll admit that yourself. I guess I just have to get used to it, and I'll try, Mums. Honest, I will."

She looked uneasily at her mother, then, with the procedure that was usually successful, changed the subject.

"Um-m-h! It smells good! Let's eat. I'll make like a bear and put my paws right in, if we don't start soon." Still there were no smiles from Mums. She tried again. "See the fancy table Aunt Martha has set for us, white cloth, flowers and everything, even if it is in the kitchen. Come on, Mums. I'll dish it up. Service!"

Mrs. Lane roused at that. "Mart's been so good," she said. "And everything will spoil from standing."

She moved toward the stove. Georgia, in spite of her quick offer of service, forgot it promptly as her mother took charge and brought the food to the table, where Georgia had already slid into her chair.

"Country chicken," Mrs. Lane said. "And homemade bread. When have I had any of that?"

Georgia looked over the table. "Plums," she said, "and chocolate-frosted cake. My Auntie Martie must be a good cook."

"She's a good cook, and a good friend," said Mrs. Lane.

Georgia's response to that was a gracious: "I won't fight with Vee, Mums. But I do think he feels a little too cocky for his own good."

"For your good, you mean," said her mother. "When we finish supper, we'll stack the dishes, and take a quick tour before we wash them. It will be too dark if we wait."

"Don't we have lights in this—house?"

"Not by touching a button. And I'd rather see it by daylight, anyway. It does seem strange without Aunt Susan. I miss her."

"Why did she pick you out to leave the place to, Mums? Wasn't she great-aunt to anybody else, too?"

"I was named for her. That had something to do with it. And we were fond of each other. Some of the others thought she was old-fashioned and queer."

"Was she?"

"Maybe, a little. But I didn't think so. I liked her, always."

With the dishes in neat piles on the drainboard beside the old-time black iron sink, they turned away to begin the "tour." The kitchen was warm from the fire in the wood stove, but the farther they went from that warmth the more chilly it grew.

"It's cold, Mums. We ought to have the heat on."

"There's no such thing as 'the heat' in houses like this one. There are stoves, and, if you're lucky, a fireplace somewhere. I don't think this house has one. This is the living room, or as Uncle Joshua used to call it, 'the settin' room.' See, it has a parlor stove."

"The room's much too small to have that thing sticking out into the middle of it," said Georgia. "There must be some better way to keep warm."

"We won't have to face that problem much until fall. The sun comes in here, and it's almost summer anyway."

"Doesn't feel like it." Georgia shivered. "Where's the dining room?"

"There isn't any, but you're used to that in Kendall Street."

"A whole house, and no dining room?"

Mrs. Lane looked amused as she answered: "Who would think you had lived for ten years in not much more than one room for everything? But come along. It will be dark before we know it."

They were standing now in the tiny front hall, with their backs toward the front door with its sidelights, and were looking up the smallest, steepest flight of stairs Georgia had ever seen. But the stairway had a mahogany rail, with a newel post at the foot. For the first time Georgia showed a faint sign of enthusiasm.

"They're cute," she said as she looked up. "Like dollhouse stairs."

Her mother was already opening the door at the right of the hall. "They couldn't spare much room for halls and such," she said. "See the parlor, Georgia."

Georgia followed, to look over her mother's shoulder. "Horrors!" she said. "I calls it gloomy. Put up the shades, Mums. Or let me."

"Yes," said her mother a little sadly. "They'll have to go up, though they wouldn't if Aunt Susan were here. This could be a lovely room, with its four windows and the morning sun. But just now I think you're right. I calls it gloomy, too. Haircloth and mourning wreaths. I wouldn't be surprised if Aunt Susan had the only room like this left in Washington County. But she wouldn't have a thing changed from what it had been in her grandmother's day."

"We can change it, can't we, Mumsie?" said Georgia eagerly. "What have I been taking interior decorating for?"

"Yes, we can change it. Let the sun in anyway."

They closed the door on the parlor, and Georgia took the steep stairs at a run. "Where are you, Mums?" she called as she looked back from the top. "Want a hand up the ladder?"

But Mrs. Lane's answer came from another direction. "I never did like those front stairs," she said, "so I'm coming up the back ones." Then she appeared, already up, in one of the rooms opening from the narrow landing where Georgia stood.

"Gee," said Georgia. "No dining room, but they had front and back stairs."

"The front ones for style and you might say for the dignity of the house, the back ones for comfort. You wouldn't call those a ladder."

She waved a hand to indicate the room in whose doorway she stood. "This used to be my room, when I came to stay over night or for a week in summer. Come in."

It was almost dark by this time, and they went quickly through the three bedrooms.

"I thought you said there was a big family. Where did they put them when night came?" asked Georgia.

"Oh, there's another bedroom downstairs that you didn't see, and the boys used to sleep in the ell, under the rafters, in what we always called the porch chamber. This is an old house, and a good many big families have been tucked away in it. Now choose your room, for tonight anyway. Mart has made up the beds, so we don't have to do that."

"I'll have the one you used to have," decided Georgia. "I think it will be the warmest, because it isn't so big." And she shivered again.

"Fine. And I'll take the west one, where we might have seen the sunset if we had come upstairs first. Now let's get back to the fire."

It was when they had the dishes done and were putting them away in the kitchen cupboards that they found the note. It was fastened to the back wall of the cupboard with a thumbtack, and was addressed simply, "Susie."

"Look, Mums," said Georgia when she spied it, "does that mean you or Aunt Susan?"

"It's her handwriting, daughter, and I think it must be meant for me." She pulled it loose from the wall, and tore open the sealed envelope.

Georgia waited in silence, till her mother had finished reading. Then she asked, "What is it, Mums? Anything important?"

"Yes, to me anyway. Here, read it."

"Why, it's dated three years ago," Georgia said.

"I noticed that. She was getting ready to go as far back as that. I should have come home long ago to see her. I wish I had."

Georgia was reading rapidly down the long page. "She knew how you felt about her, Mums. And she knew why you didn't come. She says so. And listen! 'Open it up, and throw out the old things I never could bear to part with. I'm a hidebound old woman, but you'll make the house a home again, you and your girl. And always believe in George—but I know you do.'"

She dropped the letter on the table. "Do you, Mums? Did you ever have the slightest doubt? Can I believe in him, and be sure?"

She watched her mother's head lift proudly. "Never a doubt, daughter. He wasn't that kind of man." She reached out her hand for the letter, and her eyes grew soft. "Aunt Susan might have clung too much to the past, but she was a wise woman in spite of it. She knew what I needed, and she has brought me home."

For a moment Georgia shared her mother's feeling, then she stirred uneasily. "Home to you," she said with a sigh, "but so far to me it's nothing but a roof over our heads. And I want more than that."

"Then make it more than that," said her mother with a touch of hardness in her voice. "That's up to you. Now we'll go to bed. Tomorrow will be here soon enough."

Taking a small kerosene lamp from the narrow shelf behind the kitchen stove she touched a lighted match to the wick, handed the lamp to Georgia and took up for herself the one they had used during the dishwashing. "Don't forget your suitcase. It's over there by the door."

Georgia started toward the back stairs, then stopped suddenly. "Pom," she said. "I forgot Pom. Where did she go?"

"Look behind you, in Uncle Joshua's chair."

Georgia set the lamp and the suitcase down and went to kneel before the round ball of white fur on the old chair cushion. Pom stirred sleepily, and began to purr as Georgia's hand touched her.

"Is it really Pom, Mums, or one of her great-great-grand-children?"

"It's really Pom, Georgia. She is ten this summer. Something for you to come home to, after all. Pom was yours."

"I remember her best of anything—almost. But she was a baby then, and now she's an old cat."

"Cats don't show their age. It would be nice if people were like that."

"Some people are, more than others. You don't look old, Mums."

"Me?" Georgia thought her mother looked startled. "Well, I hadn't really thought I was old," she said. "You see, I've got a lot of things to do before I step off and leave the house to you."

"Mums! I didn't mean old, like that. I just meant—"

"You meant I wasn't sixteen. Lucky I'm not, probably. But I need some youth in my veins to do my job."

"Your job! You haven't got a job now," Georgia said emphatically.

"Yes, daughter, I have a job, and you have a job, too. Somehow between us, we have to make this a home, not just a roof. Think we can do it?"

For that moment at least, Georgia rose to meet the challenge. "Sure we can, Mums. I'll try, honest I will. I've got Pom, and," rather shyly, "I've got you. That makes it a home."

"Thanks a lot. That helps. And, Georgia—"

"What, Mums?" Somehow Georgia sensed that what was coming was important. "What is it?"

"Don't ever doubt your father. And try not to mind what people look and say. They just don't know. We do."

"Yes, Mums." But Georgia's voice was faint. Nobody knew, she thought, how she dreaded meeting Lane's Cove. And how could she help that?

She picked up the lamp again, and the suitcase. " 'Night, Pommie," she said. "Come on, Mums. I hope there's a lot of blankets. It felt like winter upstairs."

The room she had chosen for the night looked a little dismal to her in the flickering half light from the little lamp. The wallpaper was one of those grayish tans that seem to catch all of the shadows and have no light to throw back. The bed and bureau were old-fashioned, but not of the heavy black walnut era like those in the Allerton house. These were painted, and had scroll-like designs and pale flowers on the low headboard of the bed, and on the bureau drawers.

Georgia had a vague memory of hearing about "Early American" in her interior decorating class. Perhaps this was it. She wished she had made more notes and paid better attention in the class. And she had a homesick feeling as she pictured Lorraine going on Saturday mornings without her.

There wasn't any bathroom, she remembered with distaste, and that feeling was not in the least lessened as she turned to face the washstand on the opposite side of the room.

"How does anybody clean her teeth in a place like this?" she sputtered aloud, and wished she had not said it when she heard the answer with a muffled laugh from the west room. Water in the big pitcher, china bowl, toothbrush mug, and slop jar.

"And after that, what?" she said a little crossly, in spite of her good resolutions. "Does the dirty water get spirited away in the night?"

"Not exactly." The laugh was not even muffled this time. "You take it away in the morning, and return the jar clean for another using."

"Good grief! What a system!" she muttered, and longed for the tiny inconvenient bathroom in Kendall Street.

The bed was comfortable, she decided when she had crept in, shivering, and settled herself under the covers. It had been a long day, and she was tired. But suddenly she realized that another hurdle lay between her and sleep. There was no light switch within reach of her hand. The hateful little lamp was still burning across the room on the painted bureau, and she had to get up to blow out the light.

Was that what you did—blow it? Or would blowing make it explode in your face? What did you do with lamps, anyway? And meekly she inquired, "Mums, how do I get the light out?"

"I'll do it this time," said her mother. "I'm not in bed yet." And she came in to lean over the bed and say, "I hope it works out, daughter. We must try to make it."

"Yes, Mums."

But she wondered, as she lay in the dark, would it? Could anybody make Hackmatack Point work out for her, and could anybody find the answer to the scornful questioning she would see in Lane's Cove eyes? She wished tomorrow would never come.

CHAPTER 5

FACING THE MUSIC

Tomorrow came, in spite of Georgia's wish that it would not. Came bright and early, with sunshine and a typical Hackmatack Point breeze. At least that is what Georgia heard from her mother, who called the information from the west room while she was dressing.

Georgia pushed one foot experimentally out of bed, and drew it back with a shiver. "Am I always going to freeze here?" she complained.

"Well, after all," her mother answered, "it's still April, and you can't expect too much of April anywhere."

Georgia could hear water splashing, probably in a huge china bowl like the one whose acquaintance she had made last night. Hers had great roses on it. She wondered what Mums' was like.

"You don't have to hurry," said her mother. "I'll go down and start the fire. Then maybe I'll bring you some warm water, this first morning. After that—"

"After that the deluge," said Georgia, "with water just above the freezing point. No, I'll take my medicine, this morning like all the others. Go along, Mums. I'll be down."

Breakfast was cozy in the warm kitchen, and after it Georgia had more courage to face the day. She opened the door and stepped out into the sunshine.

"Mums," she called back, "it's warm out here. It really is."

'Of course. It's a wonderful day. Look at the bay. See how it glitters with the sun on it."

"I'd rather it was the sun on the Charles," Georgia answered, "with me walking down the Esplanade on the way to the subway station."

Lorraine would have to take the familiar walk alone this morning. Would they miss her at the interior decorating class, and Monday morning at school? Lorraine would. She was sure of that.

Back in the kitchen, she picked up the dish towel and began to wipe the dishes her mother was stacking up in the drainer. There was something pleasant in the feel of the clean hot saucers and cups. Wiping dishes wasn't so bad. She wouldn't care much about washing them, though, even if Mums didn't seem to mind it.

"Now let's get the beds done, and then we'll be ready when Vee comes for us," Mums said when the last dish was back in the cupboard.

"Vee? What for? Where are we going?"

"To the village. Uptown, Aunt Susan used to say in the days when she went places. We have to lay in supplies. Mart started us, and we can always have milk and eggs and butter from the Allen place. But the other things we have to get at the store."

"The store? Is there only one?"

'Two or three. I don't really know about it these days, but we'll find out. Come on, the beds."

Georgia's bed was still tumbled as she had left it when she dashed out into the chilly morning, and the room looked even more dismal in daylight. No morning sun came in this window, and the drab wallpaper looked drabber than ever. As she pulled sheets and blankets into place, Georgia found herself picturing pink rosebuds on a white ground for the walls, with a frilly dressing table where it would catch the best light, and ruffled curtains to match at the one window.

If this room was Early American, she wanted none of it. Would Mums let her change it? Or perhaps this wasn't the room she wanted. She would look at the others. She was still straightening the pillows and drawing the thin old candlewick spread over them when she heard the rattle of the car turning into the driveway.

"Mums," she called, "do I have to go? How about my staying here to keep house while you buy things?"

The answer was a little slow in coming.

"If you really want to, but it isn't any use to put it off. Sooner or later, you have to face the music. It might as well be today."

"Okay, Mums." But there was no lightness in the tone, nor any in Georgia's thoughts, as she came down the steep front stairs and on through to the kitchen. Mrs. Lane was already outside and Georgia followed her to the driveway.

"Hi, kid," said Vee quite casually, as she approached. Not a bit as if he never saw me before yesterday, she thought. And without waiting for a word from her went on: "Bet you're wanting to drive the old bus. The girls I take out always are."

Georgia felt a surge of yesterday's antagonism. "You're not taking me out," she said. "You're taking *Susie*," with a heavy emphasis on the name Vee should not be privileged to use.

Vee greeted that with a loud laugh. "One on me," he said. Then he turned to her mother. "Do I have to say Mrs. Lane, when I've heard Ma call you Susie ever since I can remember?"

He sobered a little. "You'd be surprised to know how much she talked about you. She always hoped that someday you'd come back."

"And here I am," said Mrs. Lane. "I don't mind if you say Susie. Sometimes in Boston I used to miss that. There was no one to know or care whether I was Susie or Mehitabel."

"You might at least," said Georgia, "make him put an Aunt in front of it."

"So I might," said her mother. "But you'll be lucky if you don't hear somebody call me 'Suze.' It has been done."

They were at the entrance to the Allens' driveway by this time, and Vee swung the car into it and up to the back door. "Ma thought she might go too, if she got her churning done. We'll stop and see."

"Mart's a busy woman these days," said Mrs. Lane. "I haven't seen the children yet. Are they around?"

"The kids? Gone off on a school picnic—well, not a picnic exactly, because it isn't outdoors. But they're gone anyway. That lets Ma out. Saturday's one of her worst days when they're home. Always underfoot. Ma!" he called loudly. "Coming?"

The door opened sharply and Mrs. Allen came out, with the red hair still ruffling about her face and the same bright smile. She settled herself into the back seat and they started off again.

Georgia listened idly to the conversation behind her, when Vee was not talking, which he did most of the time. But finally, getting nothing but monosyllabic replies, even Vee's lively tongue ran out of things to talk about, and the back seat had it all to itself.

"—begin school Monday?" Georgia heard, and instantly her attention sharpened. Were they talking about her?

Yes. Mums was answering, as smoothly as if she were just saying she would buy a loaf of bread: "I think she'd better. There's still nearly two months of school, and she mustn't lose her promotion at the end of the year."

"Oh, no," Georgia began, then stopped abruptly. There was Vee beside her, ready to put in his two cents' worth. She wouldn't talk about it now, but when they got home again—

It wasn't as easy as that, however. Vee must have heard her muttered "Oh, no," because he was already answering it. " 'Course she's going Monday." With that wide-open grin. "Be ready, little George," he went on. "I'll show up at eight-thirty, on the dot. Have to pick up Mona and Curt Kennedy, after I get you."

"You don't have to get me," said Georgia coldly. "I think I won't start till fall."

"Won't start till fall?" Vee's eyes opened widely, and Georgia couldn't help looking into them. How blue they were! "Gosh to glory, little George. You don't know what you're bucking up against. You don't know Old Ear Muffs." For a moment he gave all his attention to the car while he eased around a huge truck that loomed up out of nowhere, then he turned back to Georgia. "You can't do that!" he said.

"What's to prevent?" said Georgia, though deep down inside she knew that there was still Mums to cope with. Mums meant her daughter to have an education. She didn't mean her to lose a year.

"What's to prevent?" echoed Vee. "Old Ear Muffs. He's a bear about losing time. A school year's a school year to him, so many weeks, so many days, and he can add and subtract like a lightning calculator."

"So what?" said Georgia.

Vee echoed her again. "So what?" he said. "So every day

you lose you make up, or you don't go ahead. You'll never get by him. You'd better be on hand Monday, if you don't want to repeat a year."

"Old Ear Muffs!" said Georgia. "I guess I don't speak your language."

"Oh," grinned Vee. "Forgot you wouldn't know. That's Chet Lindsay, high school principal. We all like him," he added, "even if we do call him names. Ears stick out like handles on the sugar bowl, or like what we call him—ear muffs."

Georgia was still puzzled. "Susie—Chet," she said. "Does everybody call everybody else by his first name?"

"Mostly," answered Vee carelessly. "But we don't say 'Old Ear Muffs' where he can hear us." The grin again. "Don't think he'd stand for that."

Coming up the little hill from the bridge across the cove, they were suddenly in the center of the town. It was a small center, with stores and post office grouped about the square where Hill Street entered Main. Vee slowed up.

"Ken's first, or Tillie's?" he asked.

His mother turned to Mrs. Lane. "I have to go to Tillie's. I hear he's got sneakers, children's sizes, and I just have to have two pairs. Let's go there first."

"Tillie's still in business, then," said Mrs. Lane. "He must be getting old, though."

"Looks just the same as he always did. And the store looks just the same, too. Sort of a hodgepodge of everything, but he most always has what you want." The two women were getting out, but Georgia held back, until Vee said, "Come on. What are you afraid of?"

"Afraid? What should I be afraid of?" she said, and was

there to enter the store close behind the mothers, with Vee bringing up the rear.

The store looked tiny to Georgia, used to chain store supermarkets. An elderly man behind the nearest counter peered at them through his glasses. " 'Lo, Mart," he said. Then, leaning forward, "Who's this you got in tow?"

He came nearer and Georgia could see his face change as he recognized her mother. "Susie Burnham, as I live," he shouted. "I'd a-known you anywhere, if it is half a lifetime since you've showed up round Lane's Cove."

He came from behind the counter, with his hand out. "Well, I am glad to see you, Susie. For sartain, I am. Thought sometimes you'd never come back at all. Wouldn't a-blamed you, either. But I guess I guessed wrong that time." He was pumping Mums' hand up and down and beaming at her, while Georgia watched from behind, relief from the fear she had denied to Vee making her weak in the knees.

What had she been afraid of, anyway? Had she expected to have people fling epithets at them and rake out the old scandal to confound them everywhere they went? Probably Mums was right, the old ones were all dead, and the rest had forgotten.

Tillie was still talking. "Staying with Mart, are y'?" he said. And before Mums could speak, he was answering his own question. "No, Tillie," he said. "Blasted numskull! Clean forgot Aunt Susan Burnham left you the place on Hackmatack. Come for all summer, maybe. Fine! fine!"

Mums was just as glad to see Tillie as he was to see Mums, Georgia thought. She herself had never heard of Tillie before. What a funny name for a man! And what a funny store Tillie kept! Hodgepodge was a good name for it. She looked around, as other customers came in and, while the others waited, Tillie turned his attention to getting the sneakers for Aunt Martha and then to filling the long list of groceries Mums produced from her purse.

A lanky boy appeared from somewhere to take care of dungarees for one man, salt pork for another, ice-cream cones for a bunch of giggling children with pigtails and short-skirted ginghams. The next customer demanded "over-hauls," but the boy merely shook his head, with "Ain't come in yet. Next week, maybe." Then raising his voice, "That right, Tillie?" to which Tillie absently answered: "Guess so. What you talking about anyway?"

People were coming and going around Mums and Aunt Martha, every now and then one of them stopping for surprised greetings when Mums was recognized. Sometimes Georgia came in for inspection. "She's certainly a big girl, Susie. I remember her when—"

Nobody mentioned her father, but perhaps that was the way people did, when you'd been dead for ten years. She remembered that she and Mums didn't talk about him often, though she knew now that Mums had not forgotten. How could she forget? Perhaps none of these people had forgotten either.

When Vee had carried out cartons filled with food—rice and beans, flour, molasses and things like that—and had put them into the back of the car, they all walked across the street to "Ken's." K. N. Morrison, the sign said. Georgia looked over at the store they had just left. Tilson Wheelwright, General Store. So he had a name, not just Tillie. Would Ken be glad to see Mums, too?

They went in, and Ken was glad to see Aunt Martha, the way storekeepers are glad to see good customers. But he didn't know Mums. Probably he hadn't lived in Lane's Cove ten years

"Well," said the man, with an unpleasant smile, "so you did come back, finally?"

ago. Georgia wondered if he had heard about the money the bank had lost. Would he think, "Lane. Oh, yes, her husband was the man—"

It didn't take so long at Ken's, and they were all moving toward the door when a man and woman came in. The woman was in a light print dress under her coat, like Aunt Martha, and the man in overalls. A little shabby, both of them. And they did know Mums. Georgia caught the surprised look in their eyes.

Neither of them paid any attention to Aunt Martha, though they must have known her, too, but came straight to Mums. "Well," said the man. "Did come back, finally, didn't y'? Guess 'twas my Aunt Susan's place that brought y'. Couldn't pass that up, Suze." His smile was definitely unpleasant.

"Hello, Herb," said Mums. Maybe nobody but Georgia could sense the hardening in Mums' voice, but Georgia could. She went on talking, smiling a little nervously. This was no friend of Mums', Georgia knew.

"She was my aunt, too, Herb. Maybe you've forgotten that." Then she turned to the woman. "Hello, Liza. It's nice to see you again. It's been a long time."

But Herb showed no intention of letting the conversation get away from him to Liza. Georgia could see that, as he elbowed forward between Liza and Mums. "Maybe so, Suze," he said. "She was relation to you, but I'm a generation nearer. Your great-aunt, but my *aunt*. Marm's own sister. Got a little weak-minded in her old age, or she'd a-remembered that. Besides, what did you need—"

It was Liza who broke in there. "Shut up, Herb," she said, in a soft voice that went strangely with her words. "And don't you mind him, Susie. He's got what the books I read call an ob-session, about Aunt Susan's old place." She laughed comfortably. "Lord knows I wouldn't want to live on Hackmatack. Suits me on the state road, where I can see the passing."

The conversation stopped abruptly with that. Herb moved off toward the back of the store, the kerosene can he carried clanking a little as he went. Liza gave Mums a reassuring pat on the arm as she followed. "Herb always did want something for nothing," she said. "Main trouble with the old coot." But she laughed as she said it. She wasn't taking Herb seriously, it would seem, even if he did take himself that way.

Georgia had watched all this with growing apprehension. Herb wanted the place, wanted to snatch away the roof from over their heads. Was that what they had come to Lane's Cove for?

Liza didn't mean to let him, she felt sure. Could he do it, anyway? There must have been, there was, a will. She looked at the stubborn set of Herb's head. Where had she seen that before? And suddenly she knew.

Herb was the "old man" she remembered in the post office so long ago. He hadn't been an old man. He wasn't that now. But when you're six all grownups seem old. *"Wonder how much of it the wife got?"* That was what he meant just now by "You didn't need—" before Liza had so promptly shut him up.

Here it was, what Georgia had been looking for ever since she had first known that she had to live in Lane's Cove. *"That there's George Lane's kid."* And now there was more to it. *"My aunt—Marm's own sister—weak-minded in her old age."* There was such a thing as breaking a will. You took the case into court. She had read about it in the Boston paper. Was that what Herb would try to do?

They walked across the street to the car, still parked by the side of Tillie's store, and while Vee packed the purchases from Ken's in the back, the others got in and waited silently. But when the car was started and going back down Hill Street toward the Cove Bridge, Aunt Martha began to talk.

"Now, Susie," she said, "you ought to know Herb Small by this time. Most of the fun he gets is in thinking what he ought to have that he hasn't. Wasn't for Liza, he'd be in hot water with somebody all the time. But she knows how to handle him. He won't try to do a thing."

"There isn't anything he can do except talk," said Mums.

"Well," said Aunt Martha, "you might as well know that he's done a lot of hunting, claiming there was a later will. Of course we know there wasn't. Aunt Susan talked up to the day she died about your having the place, and about Vince's having the will safely put away. But Herb's been after the keys, to search the house, two or three times. Kept coming, seemed to think I'd change my mind and give them to him."

Georgia listened for Mums' answer, but there was none. Aunt Martha hesitated a minute, then went on slowly. "And he's dragged up the old bank affair, too. He would! There weren't ten people in the whole town who hadn't forgotten it until he began to talk."

"And now they're all talking?" Mums' voice sounded strained.

"Well, some. I wanted Brother Tom to tell how you sold the house to cover the bank's loss, but he said that wouldn't help. They'd say that proved the whole thing. And he said everybody knows Herb Small, and that what he says doesn't count. But I wish Liza could put a muzzle on him. Liza's all right."

"Yes, she always was," said Mums. "I've always wondered how she could put up with Herb."

"Well, she does. Laughs at him, mostly. They get along."

For the first time Georgia saw how much more her mother might suffer from the old suspicion than she herself could ever do. Her own memory of her father was vague and shadowy. It would be her pride only that was hurt. But Mums!

And yet Mums had come back, and it would be Mums who had to face it all, and to make a home here, in spite of what people would say, and think.

"Mums," she said suddenly. "Don't you care! There isn't any other will, and we still have the roof over our heads. And about Daddy, all we have to find out is who did do it. Did anybody ever try?"

"Plenty!" That was Vee entering the conversation. "But nobody ever found out anything. Maybe 'the old coot' did it himself."

"Vee," said his mother sharply. "Don't go tossing out ideas like that, with nothing at all behind them."

"Okay, Ma. 'I shot an arrow into the air,'" he said jauntily. "Didn't really mean a thing, but I wish somebody'd get something on Herb Small, just once. Shut him up for keeps, maybe."

"Don't count on that, son. Herb'll be stirring up trouble as long as there's breath in him. He gets an audience that way. Only way he can. And, Susie, he knows he'll never get the house. He just likes to feel abused."

They turned at the white schoolhouse onto the Hackmatack road.

"That little thing isn't the high school, is it?" asked Georgia.

Vee's laugh was as loud as ever, she found. "That? No, that's where the little kids from Hackmatack and the Bay go.

High school's right in the center of town. Serves three towns," he said proudly. "You'll see it Monday."

Georgia's impulse was to say again, "I'll wait till fall." But she thought of Mums, and of Herb, and that people were talking, "some." Mums was right. They couldn't hide away in the gray house on the Point. "Okay," she said. "I'll face the music. But Herb Small'd better look out. I'm on his trail."

CHAPTER 6

TAKEN FOR A RIDE

Saturday afternoon Georgia was full of ideas about "finding out who did it," but one by one she gave them up. After all, it had happened ten years ago, and whoever got the money probably hadn't lingered around to be caught.

Unless he had been someone right there in the bank, and had covered his tracks so well that he could stay there and not be suspected. She would ask Mums about the bank, and she went to look for her.

"Where is the bank, Mums?" she began when she found her, standing by the south window in the living room, looking down across the wide field to the thick woods beyond.

"The bank?" her mother echoed, seeming to bring back her thoughts with an effort. "Why?"

"I didn't see anything that looked like one," said Georgia. "Isn't it here any more?"

"Yes, it's still here, but you won't find it looking very much like a bank. That's probably why you missed it. It's only a branch of the bank in Bangor, and it's a tiny little building like a box, between Tillie's store and the post office. You must have seen it."

"That? I thought it was a cobbler's shop, or something. Was that what Daddy was cashier of?" She looked distinctly let down.

"A bank is a business, daughter, not a building. And you can see that Lane's Cove wouldn't need anything very big. In fact, that little place takes care, or used to, of the bank business for three or four towns."

Georgia moved over to stand beside the window too, but she was not looking at the view. Her mind was all on the bank.

"How many people worked there? I mean when Daddy was there."

"You mean, when the money was taken. One other man, and Alice Soames, who kept the books. And neither of them took it, if that's what you're thinking."

"How do you know? And if they didn't, and Daddy didn't, who did?"

"You mean, who had a chance to do it? That's the question that nobody could answer. Tom Phillips, the assistant cashier, didn't, because he was at home sick, that day and three days before that. Alice Soames didn't, because—well, because Alice wouldn't have had nerve enough to steal a nickel, not to mention ten thousand dollars. And besides, Alice was the one who found it was missing, and nearly had what my mother used to call 'a conniption fit.'"

"Did Herb Small have anything to do with the bank?"

Mrs. Lane laughed at that, and shook her head. "No, Herb isn't on the suspect list. He never believed in banks and would have nothing to do with any of them. He had his fun, a kind of bitter fun, after the money was gone, saying, 'I told you so,' and 'See what you get for letting them have your money to play with.' But there's no reason to connect him with the loss."

"I wouldn't trust him," muttered Georgia. "Where was he that day?"

"Liza could probably tell you. I don't know. And you might as well ask that question about anybody in town as about Herb. You don't like him, that's all."

"What are you defending him for, Mums? When he's trying with all his might to take this house away from us?" Georgia asked.

"All his might is mostly talk, I'd guess, and nobody minds much what Herb says. If I were you, daughter, I'd forget trying to find out who took the bank money. Smarter people than we are had to give it up. Don't forget that the bank in Bangor was just as anxious to find out as we were here, and they never accused your father of anything. They never accused anybody. What we have to live with here is idle talk, people like Herb who always talk too much, and we have to learn not to notice it. Now let's open up the parlor."

The afternoon sun was still bright and warm, and though the parlor windows faced to the east and north, there was reflected light enough to transform the room when the shades were rolled up. In the bright light of day the room had a certain stiff charm which Georgia had entirely missed before. The hair-cloth sofa had graceful lines, and she admired the old mantel, with the big clock in the center.

"If there could only have been a fireplace under it," she said, and Mums had answered: "Maybe there is. There ought to be one somewhere in the house. Sometimes they boarded them up after stoves became the fashion and people found out how much more heat stoves gave."

She tapped experimentally on the plastered surface under the mantel into which the stovepipe was thrust. "We'll get someone who knows to look at it. There's a hearthstone anyway. A big one."

They turned away and went to the windows, curtained in stiff white lace. Pushing the curtains aside, they looked out. To the east, the road, the birches, blue water. To the north, a meadow turning green, sloping down to more water on the west.

"Water on both sides," said Georgia. "Hackmatack Point must be like a lead pencil sticking out on the map."

"Well, not quite so straight as that," said her mother. "It is narrower here than it is above or below. The water makes a nice outlook."

They left the shades up, but went back to the warmth of the kitchen fire. "Tomorrow we'll build a fire in the living-room stove," said Mrs. Lane. "The shed is full of wood, 'way up to the eaves."

Sunday seemed to Georgia likely to be a long dull day. Neither she nor her mother felt like facing the congregation at church yet. She had flashes of interest, as when her mother called her to see the downstairs bedroom back of the living room. "If we could just knock that wall down," Georgia said the minute she was in the room, "and join these two together, then we'd have a living room big enough so maybe I wouldn't mind even the stove."

"That's an idea," her mother answered thoughtfully. "I'm not sure it isn't a good idea. We'd get the sun straight through then, from the east in the morning and the west in the afternoon. And there'd be space enough to turn around in. They used to make their rooms so small."

"Well, let's do it," said Georgia. "Why not?"

"We'd lose a bedroom, though. I'd have to think. And it costs money to do things like that. We haven't much to spend."

"It ought not to cost much to tear down. No lumber, just brute strength. And we could move the parlor out here, and turn that into a bedroom. It would make a honey." She reached for her mother's hand and pulled her along through the living room and the hall to the parlor door. "Come on, we'll see where you want the bed."

"It wouldn't be so easy as all that," said Mrs. Lane, but she let herself be pushed into the room. "It would make a nice bedroom, though, and not right in the middle of the house, the way the other one is. And those two together would be a perfect living room."

She stood for a minute studying the possibilities. "But it would take more than brute strength. Plaster, and boards, paint and wallpaper, and labor. Especially labor. Go away, and let me think."

"Okay, Mumsie. But that's what you get, sending me to an interior decorating class."

"I doubt if you got all that in a few Saturday mornings. It must be some innate genius for tearing things apart. You needn't go away, after all. Where *would* I want the bed?"

But when the excitement of inspecting rooms and planning improvements had passed, the day began to drag. Georgia wandered aimlessly about, homesickness creeping nearer and nearer as hours went by.

Now, she and Lorraine would be taking their Sunday afternoon walk, maybe meeting the Roche boys somewhere on the Esplanade and walking along with them, skirting the river basin, and ending the day, after they had gone home to report, at the movies up at the Bowdoin. Did they have movies down here? Probably not.

At last, in desperation, she sat down to write to Lorraine. She had not thought she would write so soon, but what else was there to do?

Dear Lorrie: she began. *It isn't so bad, in some ways, as I thought it would be, but there's a lot could happen to make it worse. We met—*

There was a familiar rattle from the road, and the Allen car turned into the driveway. She could see Vee in the driver's seat, alone. Her first impulse was to go out to the car, or at least to the door, but she curbed it sternly. "Why should I?" she said to herself.

"Let him look for me. Maybe he's just on an errand for his mother."

She kept her pen going. *We met—a boy who lives—*which wasn't what she had meant to say at all. But it was going to be wonderful to have someone, anyone, to talk to. She held on to the paper and waited.

Vee came in with a clatter. "Anybody home round this dump?" he shouted.

"Dump? What dump? This is a house, and people knock before they burst in," said Georgia pertly. What would Vee say to that? Vee would always have something to say. He did this time.

"Sassy, eh? Thinks she's smart! City slicker awes country boy. Yeah!"

Georgia began to feel at home with Vee. This was the familiar give and take of boys and girls everywhere, the universal language.

"Did you want to see Susie?" she asked sweetly.

"I always want to see Susie. She's got a civil tongue in her head. But that can wait. I'm taking you for a ride. Come on."

Georgia wavered between showing proper reluctance, "for

Vee's own good," and making sure that she did not miss the ride.

"Has a sinister sound, taking me for a ride," she said, but she did lay down her pen and her letter and get to her feet.

They had backed out of the driveway and were well started on the road to the Corners before Vee said casually: "Stopping to pick up Mona, and then we get Curt Kennedy after that. Any place you'd like to go?"

"Yes, Bar Harbor," Georgia answered quickly.

"Too far, kid, too far. We'll go to Machias, and then maybe down to Point of Main. How's that?"

"You know I never heard of those places. So why ask me? That's what you meant to do all the time."

"Maybe I did." The grin again.

They had turned off the road into the lane leading to the Fairchild house. This was where Mona lived. Georgia hoped she would like Mona. The Fairchilds were neighbors too. The first honk of the horn brought Mona flying out from the door on a side porch, with a quick, "Hi, Vee."

"Why, she's little," gasped Georgia under her breath.

"Yeah, half-pint," said Vee. Then: "Hi, kid. In back for you today. You and Curt. Front for the stranger in our midst." And he went on to the most casual of introductions, to which Mona responded merely with "Hi." But in that one word Georgia got a definite impression that Mona was not pleased about the back seat, or about Curt, and that she and Georgia weren't likely to be friends.

"Cute," was the way Georgia reluctantly characterized her. Pale blonde hair, big blue eyes, delicate features all fitted her tiny size. "Makes me look like an ox," and Georgia considered with distaste her own more robust proportions, her less startling coloring, her brown eyes. But it really would not have mattered, if it had not been for the look in the blue eyes and that air of businesslike determination that sat oddly with her fragile prettiness.

"She gets what she goes after," Georgia thought. "But I'm not on her list of musts."

Curt proved to be as great a contrast to Vee as Mona was to Georgia herself. Shy, flushing as he mumbled his greetings, he had stowed his gangling length away beside Mona in the back, but with no visible enthusiasm on either his part or hers. Mona's conversation was all directed to Vee, and none of Vee's efforts to bring the others in made much difference. If he said, "What do you think, Georgia?" Mona was sure to answer before Georgia could get a word in. If he asked Curt a question, the answer was "Yes" or "No" without adornment or explanation. It began to be an uncomfortable ride.

"Point of Main? I should say not," Mona said emphatically. "You know very well, Vee, that I don't care about that sort of place. Islands, and bays, and points! It's bad enough to live on one." And for the first time she directed a remark to Georgia. "If I once got away from a place like Lane's Cove," she said, leaning over to look into Georgia's eyes, "no matter what made me go away, I'd stay away. Could at least live where there is something." She settled back, sputtering, "Point of Main! That's worse than Hackmatack."

They went to Machias, had ice cream at a drug store, and started back. For Georgia, they could not get home fast enough. "No matter what made me go away." That was the first dig. There would be others.

She was a little bewildered by Mona's enmity. What reason had she? Or was it enough that Mona thought she had some claim on Vee, and resented being pushed into the back seat and second place?

When at last they turned into the Hackmatack road, having dropped Curt at his door, Mona said: "I'll go down with you, Vee, while you take Georgia home, and then you can come back to the house."

Georgia looked sidewise at Vee. Would he take dictation meekly? Or was that perhaps what he really wanted to do? There was a moment of silence, then they were turning into the Fairchild lane.

"Sorry, Mona," he said as the car came to a stop. And there was no wide smile, either. "Some other time, maybe. Got a date. I'm having supper at Aunt Susan's house, with Georgia and Susie."

Georgia hoped that her start of surprise was hidden from those prying blue eyes. She turned to face Mona, who had made no move to get out, though Vee stood holding the door open for her.

"Someday, Mona," she said, "when we get settled and we get to know you better, we'll ask you down for a Sunday night. You'd like to come when Vee does, I know."

Mona's answer was delayed while she flung Vee's hand off the car door and dashed out.

"You may not get to know me better," she said then. "I'm a little choosy about my friends. My father and your father were friends, once. Then Dad crossed George Lane off his list. I'll do better than that. I won't ever put you on mine."

"Hooray!" cried Vee. "The famous temper!" And he laughed that loud laugh. "But you'll cool off before we see you in the morning. Georgia's riding with us from now on. 'By!"

Mona slammed the door, and turned her back. Georgia

clasped her hands tightly in her lap, looking straight ahead through the windshield while Vee turned the car and drove down the lane to the road. There, instead of taking the right toward the end of the Point, he went left toward the village.

"Now," he said, "we'll have a little ride. Just around the square. Let the wind blow all that out of your system. Then we'll go to your house and I'll beg that supper from Susie."

"What square?" It seemed a good safe impersonal subject.

"Oh, round through Hamlin and Woodbridge and Hayland. Then back to the Corners and down Hackmatack. Don't you mind Mona. She's always blowing a fuse when she can't get what she wants. Just didn't like the back seat, that's all."

By the time they had gone around "the square" Georgia was quite herself though she would have been glad never to see Mona again. "No matter what made me go away" and "Dad crossed George Lane off his list" kept floating across her mind. Would she be afraid of every new person she met from now on?

Vee had been talking steadily most of the time since they had turned away from the Fairchild house. Most of it about railroads, but Georgia felt sure he knew she was scarcely listening at all. She was fighting her own fight, and he was just giving her time to do it. Vee was much nicer than she had thought at first.

"—so now you see we're back in Saint Louis," he said as they went by his house and on down the road. "It made a nice trip. Fifty-five hundred miles, seeing the Grand Canyon and the Yosemite. Streamlined train, Diesel, no smoke, no cinders, keeping to schedule every second of the way. That's one thing about paper trips. But someday I'll make this a real one."

"Look, there's Pom," was Georgia's irrelevant answer. "See

her, out in the middle of the field. First time I've seen her since breakfast."

"Hunting! Busy cat. Lots on her mind." They were at the driveway now, and Vee slowed up for the turn. "Think she's glad to be home, though."

They entered the house by the kitchen door, into the warm room.

"Now," said Vee, "I've got business with Susie. Got to get asked to supper. How about it, Susie?"

"You're a fresh kid," said Georgia before her mother could say a word. "Why didn't you let me ask her to ask you?"

"No roundabout ways like that for me. What I wants, I asks for. Do I stay, Susie?"

Mrs. Lane was busy at the stove. "I was going to ask you anyway, if you had just given me time."

CHAPTER 7

CHIP ON HER SHOULDER

When Georgia woke on Monday morning she remembered first the gay supper in the kitchen last night, then the ride around the square. But after that thoughts of Mona crept in, and then the memory of Herb Small. School this morning, with Mona there, and maybe Herb's children, if he had any. There would be whispers and pointing fingers, even if there were no cruel words like Mona's. By the time she was dressed, even her new blue plaid skirt and matching blue sweater could do nothing to lighten her depression. Most of her courage to "face the music" had oozed away.

"You needn't come down here to get me in the morning," Georgia had said to Vee. "I can walk a quarter of a mile all right. I'll be there. What time?"

"Well, I suppose you can, as long as it's good weather. Eight-thirty. That gives us time enough."

So there she was, at the foot of the Allen driveway, and Vee was coming toward her in the car. "Hop in," he said, leaning over to hold the door open.

"I'll take the back this time," she said, and was in before he could answer. He closed the front door.

Then he said, "Letting Mona be boss? I wouldn't do that."

"I'm not being bossed," she said. "Back seat's fine."

"Okay, if that's the way you want it."

"Now I've offended him," Georgia thought. "But I'd rather look at the back of her head than have her staring at the back of mine."

Mona came out with the same quick dash Georgia had noticed the day before, but settled down beside Vee without a word. Georgia was carefully looking the other way. Curt joined them with only a muttered "Hi," and occupied not more than a third of the back seat, where he sat in total silence. Georgia was glad when they reached the village, turned off Main Street and she could see the school building, with boys and girls coming from both directions toward it.

The school was larger than she had anticipated, but she remembered that Vee had said it served three towns. A bus drew up and a dozen or more students exploded from its back doors. A small car labeled in large letters "School Bus" dropped a few more. Vee pulled in to the side of the road, and Mona was quick to step out and walk off without a word. Georgia braced herself for what was to come, and followed, wondering whether she had to make her way to "Old Ear Muffs" alone and introduce herself. Curt was already disappearing through a doorway on the side of the building, and Vee still had to park the car. He was saying so as it began to move. "Meet you by the office door," he added. "You wait."

Georgia had almost said, "Never mind," but was sure that he would consider that another rebuff, and, after all, at this moment Vee was her only friend. So she said, "Okay," instead, through stiff lips, and wondered if she looked as terrified as she felt.

"Silly," she scolded herself as she stood in a corner of the main corridor, waiting. "What can they do? Probably they won't even notice me, anyway." But she knew better than that, though it might easily be true in the city school she had left, where there were two thousand pupils. Here, Vee had told her, there were not quite a hundred.

When Vee came, plunging along through a crowd of boys arguing loudly in the middle of the passageway, he said: "Hey, what's the matter? You ain't—I mean aren't—going that last mile from the death house. You'll get along fine. Why not? Mona's just one, one in a hundred. She didn't like the back seat, that's all."

The office seemed quiet after the clamor outside, and Georgia almost smiled as she saw the principal at the big desk. His ears were big and they did stick out, but when Vee introduced her, she forgot the ears. Mr. Lindsay's eyes were kind, and his handclasp firm and warm.

When Vee had gone and Georgia had been seated, the principal returned to his own seat behind the flat-topped desk. "Georgia. You were named for your father, then," he said.

Georgia stiffened. "You knew my father?" she said, looking directly at him. She would go to meet whatever was in his mind.

"I knew him very well," he answered. "We grew up together, and went away together to school. Until my first job took me to New Jersey, and he came back here to work in the bank, we had never been separated. Tell your mother I am glad she is back, and that we'll be down to see her. Now, your transfer card."

The rest of the day was a blur of rooms, faces, voices, books.

"It was all right, Mums," she said when she was home again

in the afternoon. "Of course it seemed funny, such little classes. And of course they all stared. I suppose they would, at anybody new. But I can stand it, I guess."

That was to keep Mums happy. But really, she hated and feared it all. What was Mona saying to that knot of girls around her in the corridor? Did that sharp-eyed English teacher know who Georgia was? How many of the boys and girls had heard the gossip that Herb was spreading?

Mercifully, she was let alone in classes. No teacher asked anything of her that first day, and she could concentrate on getting used to the strangeness. Inwardly she looked with scorn on the small classes, contrasting them with the ones to which she was accustomed.

At recesses she kept by herself, sitting out the interminable ten minutes in the middle of the morning at her desk in the big study room, and eating her lunch there at the longer noon recess.

"There's a lunchroom, you know," a tall girl with glasses said carelessly as she dashed in to fumble in her own desk next Georgia's for paper and pencil.

"Is there?" Georgia said. "But I brought mine."

"We all do," the girl answered. "Lunchroom's just a place to eat. I'm going back. Want to come?"

Georgia shrank from facing a crowded room full of strangers. "I don't believe—" she began.

But the girl caught her up before she could go any farther. "You'd better," she said. "Get it over with. Then they can stop staring."

"Can, but will they?" Georgia tried to say it lightly, but without too much success.

"Why not? Pretty soon you won't be 'that new girl.' You'll

just be—what is your name, anyway? I'm Edwina Barrett. Funny, isn't it, Edwina? Named for my father, though. What's yours?"

Georgia took heart a little. Here was someone who didn't even know about her. "Georgia Lane," she said. "I'm named for my father, too. He was George Lane."

She lifted her head proudly and watched for Edwina's reaction to that.

There was no reaction that Georgia could see. Edwina reached down to pull Georgia to her feet. "Come on," she said. "Bring your cookies and finish down there." There was nothing to do but go.

The lunchroom was small compared to the huge school cafeteria where she had had lunches for nearly three years. But it was filled with the same sort of howling mob, she thought, as the other. They made more noise, because there were loudly shouting boys here, and she was used to a girls' school. At least the noise had a different quality, deeper and less shrill.

No one seemed to pay any attention to her, except the people at the table to which Edwina led her. "Hey," she said by way of introduction, "listen, you. The new girl, Georgia Lane." Then she turned to Georgia herself. "Nickname?" she asked. "What do they call you?"

"You can call me George. That was my father's name." She looked around and waited.

There were five girls and boys at the table, and now she saw that one of them was Vee. He moved over to make room for her on his side of the table, and as she dropped into the place he had made, she heard, under cover of the "Hi's" and "Hello's": "Now, now, little George! Why the chip on the shoulder?"

Edwina had settled down at the end of the table and spread before her the paper and pencil she had brought. "Juniors going to have a Talent Night," she explained to Georgia. Then she began her list, and Georgia forgot her own problems in watching the others. It was lucky that they weren't asking her, she thought. She was sure she had no platform talent, nor anything that could be turned into one. It was rather fun to see how some pushed for a place on the program, and others squirmed to keep from being drafted. In fact she was almost startled when the bell rang, putting a stop to everything but rushing back to study hall.

Georgia tried to figure out the plan on which the school was run. The study hall had seats for everybody, and it was there that everybody kept books and materials and to which everybody returned for study periods. Study hall was auditorium, too, with short assembly there in the morning. During the rest of the day Mr. Lindsay had classes in the front of the room, with a sprinkling of studying pupils here and there.

A teaching principal was new to Georgia's experience, but she was glad to find that Mr. Lindsay—not Chet, to her, anyway—was to be her mathematics teacher. She liked him already, and although he had not really said a word to show that he believed in her father, she felt sure he did. He and his wife were coming to see Mums.

During the ride home Mona had continued to ignore Georgia's existence, but not more than Georgia did Mona's. Vee tried to talk to both of them, and it made Georgia smile grimly to see how tangled he got in his efforts. Before they got to the Fairchild lane he had given up and there was no attempt at conversation until Mona had slid out silently and had gone off up the walk to the side door. Curt, of course, had left before that, but his leaving made no difference. He had been no more nor less silent than usual. Curt didn't count.

"Girls make me sick," Vee announced when Mona had gone and they were rattling down the road by themselves. "Why don't you get together and fight it out? Then the rest of us could have some peace."

Georgia merely shrugged. What was there to say? Once more she wished that there was some way to find out what had really happened at the bank that day so long ago. That, and that only, would be a way to fight back at Mona, and at Herb. At the whole of Lane's Cove.

But what could she do? Mums ought to do something. Mums had always found a way to take care of things that were too hard for Georgia, before. This time, all she would say was: "It's idle gossip. We have to learn not to notice it."

They were in sight of the house when it occurred to Georgia to ask Vee a question. "Who was Tom Phillips? Does he live here now?"

"Why, he's my Uncle Tom, Ma's brother. Of course he lives here. He's in the bank. Why?"

"I just wondered."

Vee looked at her, a long appraising look. "You're thinking that he might know something about that money. But if he had, he'd have said so long ago."

"I suppose he would. But, Vee, I have to find out. I didn't want to come to Lane's Cove, at all, and now I'm here I still wish I was back in Boston. But if I've got to stay here, and I suppose I have, I don't want to be looked at the way people look at me. And at Mums. I have to find out."

"What I think," said Vee emphatically, "is that nobody is going to find out, ever. A lot of water's gone under the bridge since then." They had turned into the driveway, but Georgia made no move to get out of the car, and Vee shut off the engine.

"If you've got to live here whether you want to or not," he went on, "you'd better make friends and take the chip off your shoulder. Plenty of people know what your father was like, and believe in him, but they don't know what you're like. Maybe you'd better be showing them, instead of thinking all the time about ten years ago. It's you that have to live here now."

Georgia found Vee irritating when he "aired his views." What he said made sense and she knew it did, but she turned obstinate just because she knew it. "I have to find out," she said.

"Okay," said Vee. "Hope you find out soon. Then we'll all relax."

"I think you're being definitely unpleasant. I thought you'd help me."

"I will help you," said Vee, sounding irritated in his turn, "if you'll show me what you want done. Show me a tree that's in your way, I'll chop it down. Or ask me how you get to Kalamazoo and what it'll cost, and I'll find out. But you're playing blind man's buff with something you can't catch." He stopped and drew a long breath. "What *do* you want me to do?"

"Get me a chance to talk to your Uncle Tom," said Georgia firmly, "and tell me what became of Alice Soames."

"She's dead," said Vee. "I can answer that anyway. And I'll take you to see Uncle Tom. I'll even listen while you tell me how you hate Lane's Cove and what a swell place Boston is. But I'll have my own opinion about all these things, just the same."

"So will I," said Georgia.

Vee determinedly pushed the starter, and Georgia opened the car door.

"Be seeing you," said Vee. For a second there was no sound but the rather wheezy purr of the motor. Then they both laughed.

"I suppose there's no percentage in fighting with you," said Georgia.

"No," said Vee nonchalantly. "Water off a duck's back. Why don't you put your mind on something else? Get Susie to let you tear the house to pieces, make it all over somehow. That ought to occupy even a mind set like yours."

Georgia looked at him suspiciously. "Did you hear about what I want to do to it?"

"The house?" He shook his head. "Just know that women like to move furniture, shift rooms, and things like that. Thought you'd be like the rest."

"Maybe I am. I want to knock down a wall."

Vee brightened. "Now there's something I could do," he said. "A lot better than chasing crime. When do we begin?"

"Have to let you know about that. Mums has to be convinced first. She says it costs money now even to tear things down."

"Suppose you do have to heal the wounds," Vee said. "But you'll convince her. You won't let up till you do."

"I don't convince you. 'I'll have my own opinions,' says you."

"Well, I will. It's a sort of tug of war. You pull your way, and I pull mine. But tug of war's a game, and games are fun. We'll probably keep on pulling, and having fun. Now I'd better get back up the road, or the cows'll moo their heads off at the pasture bars. 'By."

He backed the car down the driveway and Georgia watched him off up the road.

Then she went in to reassure Mums.

"It was all right." At least her words would express that Georgia hoped it was going to be, but she had her doubts.

CHAPTER 8

DEMOLITION SQUAD

The pattern of Georgia's new life was soon set, and whether she wished to or not, she had to fit into it. Riding back and forth to school every day, with Mona angrily silent and Curt shyly tongue-tied; getting used to new classes and teachers and to school life on a smaller scale; making a few acquaintances, measuring each one at first with suspicion but usually finding nothing that she could not accept.

"Chip still on the shoulder, I see," said Vee one day when he had stood by while she was definitely cool to Roland Small. "Rolie's all right. Good kid!"

"His name's Small," was Georgia's brief reply. "Is he one of Herb and Liza's children?"

"Herb and Liza haven't any children. He's some relation, but not close, I guess. And suppose he was! Herb's hipped on the subject of the house, but you don't have to be hipped on the subject of Herb. Haven't you got anything else to think about except him?"

"Plenty," said Georgia. "There's always Mona, you know. And living in a place like this. And—"

"Poppycock!" said Vee explosively. "How old are you.

seven? 'I want this,' and 'I don't want that.'" He turned off abruptly and marched down the corridor.

Georgia went to English class and tried to put her mind on "The Rise and Growth of the Short Story," on which Miss Edwards would be sure to ask for a report.

That afternoon when she reached home, Georgia found her mother sitting in Uncle Joshua's big chair by the kitchen stove. Pom was rubbing against her skirts and purring loudly as an absent-minded hand rubbed her ears.

"A penny?" said Georgia. "Or are they worth more?"

"Worth very little," said her mother, "at the moment. I haven't found the answer yet. I'm just choosing a career, like all you young things."

"Career," said Georgia. "I thought you said we could live here on what we had."

"Did I? 'A roof over our heads,' I said. And we have got that. Unless Herb finds that other will." She laughed a little.

Georgia was tense at once. "Do you think he can?"

"Nobody but Herb thinks there is one. I don't think about that. I'm thinking about the other things, more than a roof, that we need. It's poor economy to use up what reserve I have without making any effort to earn more. And the reserve won't carry us through anyway, not college for you, or the things I'd like to do to the house."

"There can't be many jobs here," said Georgia slowly.

"I'm not expecting to find a job. There might be something I could do, on my own, though. But I've thought enough for today," rising and picking up Pom. "And you haven't seen your letter from Lorraine."

Georgia jumped to her feet, seizing the fat letter her mother held out and tearing it open hastily. Instantly she was absorbed in reading, an occasional giggle alternating with a puckered frown between her eyes.

"Mums, listen," she said, and read from the letter:

"I went in to see Mrs. Allerton. I didn't think she'd answer the doorbell, so I called her up first. Her number was in the book, and she answered right away, but she didn't seem exactly overjoyed when I told her who I was.

"I could just imagine her thinking, 'So she's going to *presume,* because I let her in once.' But I was as bold as brass. I said, 'I'm coming in to see you, Mrs. Allerton.' Then I stuck 'If I may' on the end of it, very deferential, you know, and after she had recovered from the shock she said, 'Very well. Ring the bell twice.' That's what she said before. It's a kind of 'Open Sesame!' maybe.

"She was nice to me, the same as she was that night. Even if I was one of those awful people from that awful block. I didn't stay too long, didn't want to scare her. Though I have to admit she didn't seem scared. Prideful, I think would be a good word for her. As if she lived in a different world from the rest of us.

"When I said, 'Will you let me come again?' she said a kind of stiff, 'Yes, do.' And she sent a message to you. She asked where you had gone to live. She used to go to a Maine farm summers. She said so. And I told her I was going to visit you, that I had been planning to go to camp, but now I'm not. (I want you to 'set your leetle eye on that,' as Mr. Carminello says. No camp, all visit.)

"If you ask me to stay all summer, Dad says it's all right. But he hopes you have a pasture, or you won't want me that long. And he says to tell your mother I have to pay

my board, if I come for so long, same as if I went to camp.
He says to set a price, so you tell her that. High enough
so she won't lose money on me, and not so high that Dad
won't let me come."

Georgia beamed. Lorraine at Lane's Cove! She would answer the letter today. "And oh, Mums," she said, "think of
it! She got into the Allerton house again. That's Lorraine. I
wouldn't ever have had the *nerve!*"

"But, if you noticed," said Mrs. Lane, "Lorraine went to see
Mrs. Allerton, not the house. Lorraine is really a friendly person."

"Pretty soon she'll have the run of the place, and then next
we'll hear that she has Mrs. Allerton walking with her on the
Esplanade."

"Maybe," said her mother. "That would be an accomplish-
ment."

Georgia sat turning the pages and reading the whole letter
again. "Mums," she said, "we couldn't fix the new living room,
could we, before Lorrie comes? I'd like her to see the house
at its best."

Her mother smothered a laugh. "What do you care about
the house?" she said. "You called it names only a little while
ago. It hasn't changed any."

"Not yet," said Georgia earnestly. "But it's going to. You
said so yourself, and Aunt Susan, too, in the letter. Remember,
Mums? You even decided where you're going to have the bed."

"I would like to change the room. It was a good idea you
had. But first of all, we have to find out whether taking that
partition down would weaken the support for upstairs."

"One little wall like that? Oh, it wouldn't, Mums."

"Very likely not, but we need to know. And we'd have to have a man. We couldn't knock it down ourselves."

"We've got a man," said Georgia. "Or at least I have. Vee said he'd love to do it. No, I guess he didn't say it that way, but that's what he meant."

"Getting on better with Vee these days?"

"Sometimes. Other times not so good. He calls it a tug of war. He wouldn't do something I wanted him to, but he said pulling down a wall was something he could do, and when did we begin. Let's tell him, 'Right away.' "

"Don't rush me, daughter. I have to think. If I could see some money coming in, I'd feel safe and we could do a good many things."

"Lorrie's going to bring in money."

"I couldn't plan to make a profit on Lorraine. She's a friend."

"Well, let's get somebody that we can make a profit on. For the knocking down fund. Get Lorrie to bring Mrs. Allerton. She could pay, plenty."

"Aren't you moving a little fast on that, daughter? Lorrie hasn't more than got her foot in the door, so far."

"Well, that's the way you get in, or so they tell me. And Lorrie wouldn't mind giving the door a push, just a little push. Bet Mrs. Allerton's sick of staying there all alone all the time anyway. And she used to spend summers at a farm in Maine. She's stubborn. She said she would, and so she does. But Lorrie'll talk her out of that."

"And you're trying to talk me into thinking of Mrs. Allerton already established here for all summer. Did you ever hear of counting chickens before there are any chickens?"

"Yes, but if nobody ever looked ahead and took a chance, where would the world be?"

Mrs. Lane laughed. "I wouldn't know the answer to that. So let's get supper and leave Mrs. Allerton to manage her own affairs."

"Or have Lorrie manage them for her. Lorrie could."

Georgia no longer felt lonely at school, though she really knew few of her schoolmates. "Mona's crowd," as she called them in her mind, made no overtures toward acquaintance, and Georgia often had a feeling that their giggling conversations together had her as their subject.

"What do I care?" she would say, to herself or to Edwina and Mag Fletcher, with whom she usually spent her recesses. If to herself, she would perhaps add, "Only a bunch of hicks!"

But she knew by this time that "hicks" were no different, except on the surface, from herself. Vee delighted in calling her "city slicker" and probably Mona's crowd could think up worse names than that. Calling names, in fun or otherwise, was easy, but what really troubled Georgia was remembrance of the bank loss and what they might be saying about her father.

"When do you take me to see your Uncle Tom?" she asked Vee one afternoon as they were almost home.

"He's been too busy lately," Vee answered. "Annual accounting and audit. Comes this time every year. Anyway, he and Aunt Lou are coming down to see your mother. Why don't you wait till then?"

"I want to *talk* to him, not just 'How do you do? Glad to meet you.'"

"Okay. But what do you want to say? 'Did you by any chance take that money the bank lost?'"

"I don't believe you care whether I ever find out, Vee Allen. If it were your father—"

"Maybe it was," said Vee obstinately. "He was around that day."

"Around where? The bank?"

"Yeah. I've heard them tell about the accident and all the rest of it. Of course Dad's a director in the Bangor Bank anyway, and he was in the bank here when Alice found the money was gone. Uncle Tom was home in bed, with flu. Now I suppose you'll want to talk to Dad."

"Of course I'll want to talk to him. Why didn't you tell me before?"

"You didn't ask me. And besides, you get ideas enough without my putting any into your head. Let's talk about railroads, or about knocking down walls."

"We've finished talking for today," said Georgia. "Be seeing you." And as Vee brought the car to a stop, she hurried out and across the grass to the kitchen door, without a look back.

"Mums," she called. "Mums!"

"Yes?" The answer came, muffled, from somewhere below Georgia's feet. "I'm down cellar. Come and look."

"Look? What at? What's in a cellar except water pipes and a furnace?" She went over to the door standing open on the other side of the room and looked down the cellar stairs.

"Come and see. No furnace, no water pipes. Treasure. Come down."

Georgia stepped gingerly onto the bare plank stairs. "I won't go through, will I?" she asked.

"Of course not. Didn't you ever see a cellar before?"

"I don't think so," peering about the damp and dimly lighted place. "Where's the treasure?"

"Over your head. On the hanging shelves." Georgia looked up, following her mother's pointing hand.

"There's enough to feed a regiment!" Mrs. Lane exclaimed.

"Hanging shelves," she said. "Never heard of such a thing. What do they hitch to?"

"The floor beams over your head." Georgia could see now that the shelves were filled with fruit jars, all neatly labeled and showing their contents through the glass.

Her mother reached up and took one of the jars in her hand. "See!" she said. "Enough to feed a regiment. Plums, sugar pears, blueberries, raspberries, applesauce, everything. And over there," pointing to another of the heavily laden shelves, "all kinds of vegetables, lobster, clams, fish, pork, chicken. I've seen down-east cellars before, but I never saw one better stocked. Hundreds of jars."

She went over and sat on the stairs. "Aunt Susan!" she said. "All those last years she must have kept Nan Stickney putting up everything, just as if she still had a family to feed. She was getting ready for us. I wish I had come home sooner, to see her once before she died. I wish I had."

"She knew, Mums. She said so in the letter. And I bet she had fun thinking how surprised you'd be when you found all this. Don't feel bad, Mums. I'll help you make it a home. Honest, I will."

Later, back in the kitchen, Georgia said: "We won't be hungry next winter. We ought to feed more than two people, and a cat. I shall dream about it tonight, a regiment of jars, to feed a regiment of people. Lorrie and Mrs. Allerton, to start."

"I'm afraid that's nonsense," said Mrs. Lane. "You're not waiting till night to dream. Forget Mrs. Allerton, and don't go putting ideas into Lorraine's head. Hackmatack Point's not a summer resort. Most people wouldn't want to pay money to stay in this kind of place. And I don't know as I would want people, if they wanted to come."

"Well," said Georgia, "you want a career, and you've got the house. Better bring them together."

"I would like to change the rooms, and the parlor would make a wonderful room for a 'paying guest.' If I could bring myself to have a paying guest around."

"You wouldn't mind Mrs. Allerton. A little queer, maybe, but you said you liked her. Let's tell Lorrie to go ahead, follow up the foot in the door and next thing you know you'll be going with the throttle wide open, as Vee would say."

"Georgia, Georgia! How you do hang to an idea when you get it in your mind. *Forget Mrs. Allerton!* But I'm going up to see Mart after supper, and I'll ask Vince what he thinks about taking out the wall. It wouldn't cost too much, and with the cellar full of food, I think we could afford it. What a wonderful time you and Vee would have. The demolition squad!"

Georgia's mind shifted from paying guests to thinking that she would ask to go with her mother to see the Allens. If she did, when Mums had finished talking to "Vince," Georgia might get a chance to ask a quiet question or two about the bank money. But she gave up the idea. There was studying to do.

Mr. Lindsay's junior review math was something to be reckoned with, and she meant to get as good a mark as she had been doing in math in Boston. With only six in the class, you never had a chance to hide behind "He won't call on me today." He always called on everybody every day.

She laid out her books on the kitchen table, with a fleeting thought for the enlarged living room where she might soon be studying. Then she did read Lorraine's letter once more before she began to work.

"It *is* a good idea," she said aloud, "and Lorrie could do it.

See what she's done already. I hope she tries. Then Mums
would break down, the demolition squad would get to work,
Mums would stop thinking about money, and everything
would be okay. Okay! Okay!" She repeated as she attacked
the first problem. "Everything would be okay!"

But she came to herself with a sharp revulsion of feeling.
Everything would never be okay until she had solved the bank
money mystery. Then she could hold up her head with any
of them, and if anybody was going to be left off anybody's list
of friends, it would be Mona left off from Georgia's, not the
other way around.

But it was probably silly, the way Mums and Vee said it was,
for her to think she could find out what happened ten years
ago. So far, she'd found out just exactly nothing. Where were
the clues? There weren't any. If anybody in Lane's Cove
knew anything about it, and he hadn't told in ten years, he
wouldn't tell now. What kind of a dope was she, anyway?

She pulled books and papers toward her. She'd better get
at the job, or "Old Ear Muffs" would take it out of her tomorrow. She picked up her pencil, inspected the sharpness of
its point, and began to draw an isosceles triangle at the top of
a sheet she had headed, "Home Work Math" with the date.

Except for Mona and her crowd, school wasn't so bad. After
all, school was school, and math was math, in the city or in
the sticks. And she'd better be good, with "Old Ear Muffs"
around.

CHAPTER 9

THE CAMEL'S HEAD

"Mums! Mums! Come and look! It's all down but the bare bones."

Georgia danced up and down with excitement, and Vee stood with a satisfied grin in the midst of laths, plaster and general litter, still clutching the ax whose heavy head he had used, for lack of more professional wrecking tools.

"Give me the hammer, Toots," he said. "Look at those old square nails. Bet they're handmade."

Georgia automatically thrust the hammer into his hand, but her eyes were all for the spacious room that was coming into being. She could scarcely wait for the final step, removal of the rough narrow uprights that still stood like prison bars between the original rooms. Already she could see in her mind's eye the old sofa standing where the bed had been, and low bookshelves built in along the south wall.

"But there's only one window on the west side," she said. "There ought to be two, to catch all that afternoon sun going to waste, and to match the two opposite, on the front. Could we have another one? I wonder."

"Sure," said Vee, "if you had someone who knew enough to

get it in the right place, and cut it square, and all those things. Me, I'd rather lay out a trip to Alaska than try room planning. Guess you like it, though. First time I've seen you really get steamed up about anything."

"I've got to have that window," Georgia said, more to herself than to him. "I don't see why they didn't have it in the first place."

"Didn't want to heat all outdoors, likely," said Vee. "More windows, more wood to cut and carry."

"That was it, Vee," said Mrs. Lane, who had come in and stood looking at the wreckage and the "bare bones" still standing. She went over to the opening where the door between the rooms had been, and inspected the way the uprights had been fastened at top and bottom.

"Be careful, Vee," she said, "when you knock the studding down. The studs are nailed to a good solid hand-hewn crossbeam at the top, but even so don't be too reckless with your hammer and that ax."

She stepped back to get a general view, as Georgia had done, of the emerging room.

"Looks to me," she went on, "as if your job is nearly done. Then we have to have a carpenter to take up where you leave off. Who does that kind of thing here now? I've lost all track of things like that."

"Well," said Vee, with a sidelong glance at Georgia, "guess the only one you could probably get is Herb Small. Henry Layton's building a big barn over in the Lilley District, and Dan Roscoe'll be another month on the place he's putting up for those New York people down on Birch Island. That doesn't leave anybody but Herb. He gets most of the short jobs like this."

"Herb?" said Georgia explosively. "It would spoil my lovely room just to have him touch it."

"Nonsense!" said her mother. "We need a workman to do a job, and what he thinks of us doesn't matter. Are you afraid of Herb?"

"No," said Georgia. Then with a lightning change: "All right! Get Herb. In his odd minutes he can make sure we haven't destroyed a will that disinherits us, and in mine—"

"In yours you can find out what Herb's done with the bank money. Sure hasn't made any difference in the style of living down at Smalls'."

"Vee," said Mrs. Lane, "remember what your mother said about tossing around ideas that you can't back up with facts. I never did like Herb very much, but he didn't take that money. He didn't even have a chance."

"Nobody had a chance, far as I can see." He laid down the hammer and picked up the ax. "And maybe that's an idea," he went on as he struck the first blow from the back at the studding. "Probably the money wasn't taken at all. Slid down behind the bureau drawer, or something like that. Still there."

He aimed another blow. The first of the studs came away from the beam at the top and leaned out ready to fall. A blow near the bottom, and Vee caught the stud deftly as it came entirely loose. Conversation stopped and all three concentrated on the new room that every moment brought nearer. Then the last of the studs came down and the room took on length, with the barrier gone.

Georgia drew a deep breath of content. "Oh, Mums," she said, "now it's beginning to be our house. Our own house, from now on." She went to stand where the wall had been, looking first one way, then the other.

"Can't you see it, Mums?" she asked. "The sofa here, book-cases against that wall, the new window—"

"Window?" said her mother. "New window?" Then she laughed. "I see the camel has his head in the tent."

They all laughed at that. "But he's a good camel," said Georgia. "You'll like him, even when he's all in."

"I hope so," said her mother. "But I don't like all this mess to stumble over. Let's turn to and get it out. And then when Vee's so inclined he can take me up to see Herb. Well begun may be half-done, but the other half's important, too."

"I'll say," said Georgia. "I can't wait." And she started to gather up an armful of laths to carry out.

That night they went to call on Herb and Liza. "It has to be a call," Mrs. Lane said. "Liza rates a call, even if Herb might not. Want to come, Georgia? Or do you have to study?"

"I certainly don't intend to miss seeing that bozo," said Georgia. "I'll get up at daybreak to study, if I have to."

So, after an early supper, they set out. Up through the village, and east a mile or two on the state road; now they were turning into an untidy driveway leading to a shabby house.

As they approached, a friendly dog with wildly wagging tail came from one direction, Herb appeared from another, and Liza stepped out from the kitchen door, all at once. And they all spoke at once, too.

"We-e-ll, Suze," said Herb. "Come to admit the house ought to 'a' been mine?"

"Isn't this good of you, Susie, not to wait till I could get to you." Liza beamed at them from the top step, and the dog barked loudly what might have been either a warning or a welcome.

When they were in the house, Georgia was impressed at once

by Liza's tidy housekeeping. The outside might be shabby, but from the moment they had crossed the threshold everything had the look of having been scrubbed or painted that very day.

"Come into the front room," Liza said, leading them through the kitchen faster than Georgia really liked. She wanted to stop to look at the windowful of geraniums, blooming gaily against the early evening light; at the old black cookstove, gleaming with carefully rubbed on polish; at the floor of wide pine boards, innocent of any finish except the clean white from years of daily washing. "On her hands and knees," even Georgia, the city girl, recognized.

The front room was small, no bigger than theirs in Kendall Street, Georgia thought, but every inch of space was used. Hand-hooked rugs elbowed each other on the floor, crocheted scarfs and tidies, patchwork cushions on every chair. The curtains of coarse scrim showed more crochet, with borders of lace edging, and insertion set inside the hems.

"Well, you see, I have lots of time," said Liza, when Mrs. Lane exclaimed at the quantity of her work. "With only two to do for. Can't scrub every minute, but a body needs something to keep her hands busy."

"I'd think so," said Georgia to herself, "just to keep my mind off Herb."

Vee had stayed outside, playing with the dog, and she could hear Herb's querulous voice complaining about the backward spring, the scarcity of seed potatoes, the high price of grain. Nothing would ever be right with Herb, she was convinced.

Then he appeared in the doorway of the room where they were sitting. He stood there, a funny little cotton cap, with "Benton's Fertilizer" across the front, perched on the back of his head, and one nervous hand twiddling the scanty mustache which drooped over an equally drooping mouth.

"Mums has beat him to it," Georgia thought when her mother spoke, the minute his lanky shape showed in the doorway.

"Well, Herb," she said cheerfully, "I hoped you'd come in. Got time to do a job for me? We're making some improvements."

"What you doing to my Aunt Susan's house?" he asked belligerently.

"Nothing that will harm it. But we do need some help, and you know how to do the things we need done. Busy just now?"

"Nothing he can't leave," said Liza.

Herb seemed to consider the matter doubtfully. "I might make it," he said at last. "Better than have you tinkering with it. No knowing what you'd do."

"That's right," said Mrs. Lane. "I wouldn't trust myself too far with a hammer and nails. How about coming down with us now to see what we need to get before you begin?"

"Haven't said I'll take the job," said Herb. "Just said I might. What you doing anyhow?"

"Come on down and see."

"By jinks, I will. And if you're—"

Liza interrupted. "Then take off that pesky little advertising cap, and get a hat on your head. Look like a walking fertilizer bag in that."

Herb disappeared from the doorway, muttering, and Liza followed, saying apologetically: "Have to get him his hat. He wunt see it if it's bumping him in the nose."

The ride back to Hackmatack was a somewhat silent one. When the five of them had filed through the kitchen into the cleared and swept space that had once been "settin' room" on the front and "nursery" on the back, Georgia watched for an explosion from Herb. But none came. He stood for a moment just inside the door from the kitchen, then went over to examine the narrow raw opening up the two walls and across floor and ceiling where the partition had been.

"See what you want," he said. "Pretty good idea, at that."

Georgia almost gasped. Had Herb had a change of heart? She couldn't believe that, and after he had begun to speak again, she knew he had not. Standing squarely in the middle of the opening, he looked at Mums with a mixture of obstinacy and sly humor.

"What you're doing wunt hurt the house none, Suze," he said. "I can fix it up so's it'll never show a wall was there. But I give you fair warning. I still expect to find another will, and if I ever do, the house'll be mine. If you want to spend your money on it," with a shrug of his narrow shoulders, "knowing what's likely to happen, well and good. That's your risk."

"Talk sense," said Liza, still in that soft, easy voice. "Any will there was would've showed up long before this, and you'd better stop chasing rainbows here and now. Besides, we got a house, and not most out to sea like this one either."

"No law against having two houses," said Herb. "Sell one, maybe. If they's a will—"

"Like to know where that fancy will would be," said Liza.

"Might be right here," answered Herb. "Though I s'pose—"

"You suppose we'd have burned it up," snapped Georgia, unable to contain herself. "Well, we haven't."

"Kind of you to tell me," said Herb. Georgia supposed that was sarcasm, and would have liked to answer it in kind but couldn't think of anything sarcastic to say.

Her mother took up the conversation, motioning Georgia to be silent. "If you find it, Herb," she said, "maybe the house is yours. But Aunt Susan might have left it to found a home for cats. She liked cats." Somebody laughed. It might have been Vee.

Herb's temper let go. "Laugh, laugh!" he said. "But will you give me leave to hunt? What's in the old desk?"

"Nothing much," said Mrs. Lane. "It's no use to hunt. And what I want now is to get this room fixed up. What do I have to buy for you to work with?"

Herb grudgingly gave his attention to the matter of the room, and nothing more was said about the will. Everything was finally arranged, and Liza was already in the kitchen on the way out when Georgia had a sudden thought.

"Mums," she said softly, "would he know about fireplaces, too?"

"Probably," said Mrs. Lane. She turned to him. "Were there ever any fireplaces in this house, Herb?" she asked.

" 'Course there was fireplaces. What else did they have a six-foot chimney for, like to know." He went over and tapped the wall under the mantel, where the stovepipe entered the chimney.

"Hollow," he muttered. "Fireplace there, for sartain. Boarded up and plastered. Aiming to tear it out, Suze?"

"Oh, yes," said Georgia, before her mother could answer. But Herb paid no attention to her. "What say, Suze?" he urged. "I can do it, if you say the word. That wouldn't harm the house none, either. 'Course you'd probably freeze in the winter, without the stove. Or maybe you don't expect to be here winters. Live in style in Boston, maybe."

Live in style in Boston! Georgia remembered that, in the

post office, when she was six. And what he had said next. *Wonder how much of it the wife got?*

But Mums was answering him. "We can't afford to live in style, anywhere, Herb. Aunt Susan's house is all that stands between us and having no house at all. I've worked for ten years, and now I've lost my job. I've come home, and we'd like to do a few things to fix the house up. We can't afford much. We'll think about the fireplace. The others must be done."

"Spent everything, eh? Well, I suppose you would, in ten years." There was that sly look in his eyes again. "Hope you won't be fixing up the house just for me and Liza to spend our old age in, that's all. I'd feel some sorry about that."

"Would you? We'll have to take that risk, as I said. Now, did you say you'd come the first of the week, if I can get the lumber and the other things?"

Herb nodded, and went on to join Liza, who was leaning over Uncle Joshua's chair in the kitchen, with Pom purring like a steam engine under her caressing hand.

There wasn't much of the evening left when Vee went off to deliver Herb and Liza back at their house on the state road. Georgia thought at first that she would go with them, but Herb clambered at once into the front seat, and Georgia didn't feel well enough acquainted with Liza to welcome the idea of keeping up a conversation with her in the back.

So Georgia stayed at home, and laid out her books on the kitchen table as she did every night. What she really wanted to do at that moment was to write to Lorraine. There was so much to tell her, so much that she had thought she never would tell but that now clamored insistently to be told to someone. "And Lorrie's the only one who would understand," Georgia thought.

Mums had said that she must not put ideas into Lorrie's head, but surely she could comment on the fact that Mrs. Allerton had summered in Maine years ago. And how much good it would do her to get away from Kendall Street, with all its summer noise and dirt. Then somewhere else in the letter, when she had told about the changes they were making at Hackmatack Point, it would be all right to say that Mums wanted to use the house to make some money for them. And how perfect the parlor would be for someone who would pay for a summer close to the sea. She laughed a little guiltily when she got to that point in her planning, admitting to herself that that would be another camel pushing into another tent.

"Mums," she said, "let me tell Lorrie. It isn't anything that would do Mrs. Allerton any harm, and if you want to make money you have to advertise. Don't you?"

Mrs. Lane looked up from the paper she was reading. "Tell Lorrie?" she said. "Advertise? Oh, you mean have her try to get Mrs. Allerton down here. That sounds like an impossible scheme to me. A woman who has shut herself away so long—"

"I think she's tired of shutting herself away. She probably wonders why she ever did it. The parlor, I mean the parlor bedroom, would be perfect for her and by the end of the summer she'd be just like anybody. And stop hiding behind the curtains when she went back to Kendall Street. Lorrie'd fix it, if you'd let her."

Mrs. Lane answered that positively and at once. "I don't want anybody fixing anything. You may tell Lorraine that we are thinking about renting that room, with board, to someone for the summer. Then, if Mrs. Allerton is interested, she can do her own fixing. Probably she won't be interested, and will stay behind the curtains just as she has for so long. Now, you'd better get at the studying."

"I'm going to write to Lorrie first, and I'll get up early in the morning to do the homework. It isn't so cold mornings now, and I'll build the fire anyhow. I've learned that much since we came."

Georgia rose to get her notepaper, and set to work with enthusiasm on the letter. She would mail it in the morning, when they passed the post office on the way to school.

CHAPTER 10

LUCY LORENZO'S BONNET

Georgia hated the rides to and from school, with Mona either stiff and silent in the back, or gaily talkative when she sat on the front seat with Vee. In either case she entirely ignored Georgia's existence. Vee had somehow established an unacknowledged rule of alternating where they should sit.

This morning Mona was beside Curt in back, but Georgia found it hard to talk, knowing that Mona was there behind her. She held tightly to the letter she was to mail in the village, and when she stepped from the car to drop it in the slot at the post office she said, "Go ahead, Vee. I'll walk up the hill."

She could imagine how Mona would break into bright conversation the moment Georgia had disappeared. Well, let her. Who cared?

School always took all of her attention. Mr. Lindsay was a good teacher, she was sure. About the others she was not so sure, but she worked hard for all of them. Her transfer card from Boston had shown good marks, and she must not drop below that standard here.

Today in French class they were starting sight translation from a book of famous short stories. When Miss Young distributed the books, there were not quite enough and Miss Young said casually: "Mona, move over and share your book with Georgia for today. I'll get another before class tomorrow."

"Horrors!" thought Georgia, but she moved over and let Mona slip into the seat beside her. She could see the amused looks that the others in the class exchanged. Everybody knew how they hated each other, she was sure.

Perhaps because of the shared book neither of the two girls was called upon. Mag Fletcher, or Margaret as the teacher quite formally called her, was the first one, and gave a passable translation. Then Miss Young said, "Curtis Kennedy," and Curt struggled to his feet, uncoiling his long legs from the iron base of his seat.

Georgia always felt sorry for Curt in French class. She knew that her own accent was nothing to brag about, but Curt's French sounded like nothing Georgia had ever heard. And he suffered so visibly, the dull red mounting from neck to scalp, the knuckles of his big awkward hands showing white as he clutched his book.

Miss Young suffered too, it was evident, as Curt blundered through the preliminary reading of the paragraph before attempting to translate. "No, no, Curtis," she said impatiently, "I'm sure no Frenchman could possibly guess what you are trying to say." And she pursed her lips as she corrected his impossible *eu*.

"I couldn't understand him, either, if he tried to talk my language," said Curt sulkily.

It was the first time Georgia had heard him even try to defend himself against anyone. And it was comforting to know that Curt realized that he had a language. He was the sort of country boy that she had thought of as the only sort, entirely inarticulate, abashed in any group, and probably wholly at home only among the cows and horses of his father's stock farm.

Vee was quite different. No trouble there about expressing himself. But then, she thought, Vee came from a different country background. She had been silly to think that all country boys were alike. Vee loved to brag about his ancestors sometimes, she remembered. Great-grandfather, Captain Allen, one of a score of Lane's Cove captains of his day, in the China trade. In the Allen house was a full dinner set of Royal Canton china that he had brought home. Georgia had seen it.

"The Cap'n sailed out of New York for thirty years," Vee had explained proudly. Then there was Grandfather Allen, the one they called V.L., member of Congress, on the Governor's Council, "head of everything big they ever undertook in Washington County," according to Vee. And Vee's father, "Vince," Harvard College and Law School graduate, able to carry the law business of several towns, be head selectman, bank director, and have a well-kept little farm on Hackmatack besides. Vee had plenty behind him, and a ready tongue as well.

Tonight she and Mums were going to supper with the Allens. She hoped that she would get the chance to talk to Mr. Allen, who had been in the bank that day when Alice had discovered the money loss. Vee had promised to fix it somehow.

That afternoon on the way home she sat in the back seat beside Curt and for the first time she tried to urge him into speech.

"Sometimes, I wonder," she said conversationally, "how good Miss Young's own French is. She doesn't sound like my Boston French teacher. Miss Laserte really is French. Came from Paris."

She thought she heard a sniff from Mona in front. Curt actually did try to answer, but got no further than, "Beastly stuff. Got no use for it."

"Where are you going after next year, Curt?" Vee called back over his shoulder.

"Some kind of farm school, I guess." Curt wasted no words.

"I want to go in for transportation," said Vee. "Like to think about moving people and things across the country. Like trains. You know that."

Mona was evidently uneasy at having let the conversation out of her own hands and she interrupted now with: "That's enough about your ambitions, Vee. Got your tickets for Talent Night?"

Georgia thought about Lane's Cove next winter with Vee away at college. Next year she would be a senior at high school, and after that she could only guess. She wished she knew, the way Vee did, what she wanted to do. She would like, she thought, to learn about houses, especially about making them beautiful, and livable, inside. She must find out about art schools, whether they would offer anything like that. Something like her interior decorating class, but beginning further back and going further into the subject than that did.

In the meantime, there was the house on Hackmatack. The new living room would be fine, especially with the extra window. Mums had said she might have it, and that was the first thing Herb would work on today. She forgot the others and wished she were already at home, to watch the opening cut and the window go in.

When Mona and Curt had gone and Georgia and Vee were riding on down the road, she mentioned the window and said, "Want to come in and see it?"

"Can't today," said Vee. "Got a book report to turn in to-morrow, and some stiff math to do. Having company to sup-per," and he grinned cheerfully. "Perhaps the company'd bet-ter do her own math this afternoon, too. Keep clear with Ear Muffs. Safer."

Perhaps she had better, Georgia agreed reluctantly. "But I wanted to list the things to ask your father," she added. "And we're coming early, I hope."

"Think you're counting too much on Dad. Don't believe he knows a thing. And I don't think he likes to talk about it."

"I want to ask him." There was that slightly stiff obstinacy in her voice. "Do you mind?"

"Me? What for? But you're wasting your time."

"Okay. I'm wasting my time." They were at the driveway now and the car stopped. With a wave of her hand, Georgia made a quick exit. Vee backed the car out and was off up the road.

The window was already in, and was all that Georgia had hoped. There was a great temptation just to stand there minute after minute, "gloating," she admitted to herself. But she turned away and went to the desk.

Herb was on his knees by the opening in the floor where the partition wall had been, fitting in boards, shaving off a little here and piecing in a little there. "Crooked as a ram's horn," he muttered as he worked. "Didn't they ever get anything straight, or plumb?" He paid no attention to Georgia, nor, after the first glance, she to him. The only sounds in the room were the tap of his hammer and an occasional rattle of paper at the desk.

The math went well today, so that there was time left when it was done, and Georgia began to make the list of questions to ask Mr. Allen. It was queer that she did not know some of these things already, she thought. Mums must have known them. She put the list together slowly, trying to think of what else she ought to know about the day. After a while she added another question. Did Mr. Allen know where her father was going when he set out in his car? And after a longer time, still another. What did the bank directors really think about the loss? Did they blame her father?

She knew that she could ask her mother some of these things, but she hated to do so. Besides, she wanted to know exactly what Mr. Allen remembered. He must remember, even though Vee said his father "didn't know a thing."

She could hear her mother moving about upstairs, and knew that she herself ought to be freshening up and changing her dress if they were to be early at the Allens'. She laid the list down and went around through the kitchen and up to her room.

"Hi, Mums," she called. "What's going on?" and she came to stand in the open doorway of her mother's room.

Mrs. Lane looked up from a heap of miscellaneous clothing on the floor in the middle of the room. "I'm throwing away," she said. "I'm sure this must have been Lucy Lorenzo's." She held up an antiquated blue bonnet, faded in streaks and ornamented with rosettes of much more faded pink ribbon. "I've always heard that Lucy was 'dressy.'"

"Who was Lucy Lorenzo?" asked Georgia curiously.

"She was—let me see, she'd be your great-great-grandmother Burnham. There used to be a daguerreotype of her, standing beside Lorenzo, who sat solidly in the photographer's straight chair."

"Why was his name like hers?"

"Oh, her name wasn't really Lorenzo at all. She was called Lucy Lorenzo because she was Lorenzo's wife, and there was probably another Lucy in the family or having the Burnham name. I think I've heard of Lucy Ben. There was Mary Azro, and Mary Marcellus, and a whole flock of Lizas. Liza John, and Liza Jonathan, and Liza Phin. His name was Phineas. There were a good many Burnhams in those days." She twirled the bonnet on her hand. "Too bad to throw all these away," but she dropped the bonnet on the heap.

"Oh, don't, Mums. Don't throw them away. Think what a costume party they'd make."

"I suppose they would," said her mother, "but you can't have closets full of this kind of stuff. They didn't allow much room for closets when this house was built, and what space there is we need."

"Put them in the attic. There is an attic, isn't there?" Georgia had not thought of that before.

"Only a little one, out beyond the porch chamber in the ell. I haven't been out there yet."

"Put them in the—what did you call it?—porch chamber. We don't need that now. And I'll find some place for them. They ought to be in a museum." Georgia came over to lift the old bonnet, admiring the big scoop of its flaring front.

"Probably half the attics in town have things like these," said her mother. "They'd make quite a display all together."

"I'd like to see them that way." Then suddenly Georgia remembered that she had meant to ask Mums to start early for the Allens'. They must both get at their dressing or they wouldn't even get there on time for supper. She swooped down on the heap of old clothes.

"They're mine, Mums. That all right?"

"If you'll get them out of my sight, and leave me room to hang my clothes."

Georgia went toward the door into the porch chamber in the ell, her arms full. "Tonight they can stay here. Then I'll do something with them, but now we've got to hustle or we'll be late." Dumping the armful on the spool bed in the porch chamber, she hurried back and into her room.

Supper at the Allens' was a lively affair. There were eight at table, the three younger children, with clean pinafores and scrubbed faces occupying one whole side, smiling confidently at the guests opposite.

"They're all like that," Georgia thought. "Not pushing exactly, but just sure. From Vee down. It's nice to be sure," and she sighed. "But probably nobody ever said their father was a thief."

She looked at Aunt Martha, at the appetizing food, at the Royal Canton china on the table. "We don't use it all the time," Aunt Martha said, "but this is an occasion. The Lanes are back in Lane's Cove."

She was serving the children expertly, pouring milk, seeing that they had bread and butter, dishing out applesauce. Uncle Vince, as Aunt Martha had said Georgia must call him, cut thin slices of country-cured ham, spearing crisply browned potatoes to lay on the plates, with vegetables that Georgia guessed came from hanging shelves in the cellar, like those in Aunt Susan's house.

"I must stop calling it Aunt Susan's," she thought. "It's ours now, the way she wanted it to be. Like ours at home," she amended silently but firmly.

By the time dessert came, there was general talk and laughter, and under cover of the noise and chatter Georgia took opportunity to study Uncle Vince. Was he going to help her as she had hoped? After supper she would know.

Vee wasn't a bit like his father, she concluded. Uncle Vince was dark and quiet, telling his stories with a slow drawl, and without a vestige of a smile. Had the old "Cap'n" been like him, or like Vee? Like Vee, probably. It had to be someone who was sure, to sail all over the world, to command rough men and deal with strange people. Vee would love to do all those things, she felt certain. Or to do the things he had told her about the one they called V.L., Vee's grandfather. Making speeches in Congress, commanding men in the Civil War, digging his way out of Libby Prison with a spoon. They still had the spoon, Vee said. She must ask to see it.

No, Uncle Vince looked a softer sort than that. He'd be a kind and gentle friend. But she couldn't imagine him in command. It was after supper, when Mums and Aunt Martha had driven everybody else out of the kitchen, that Vee took her in to talk to his dad.

"Come on," he said. "Dad's smoking his pipe and ought to be feeling well fed and amiable. Good time to tackle him."

"He looks as if he'd always be amiable. I think he's going to be easy to talk to," said Georgia as they crossed the living room and entered a small cluttered room with a big cluttered desk.

"Here she is, Dad. Says she wants to talk to you."

"Well, that's good. Sit down, Georgia. Your father was my best friend."

That was a fine opening for her, Georgia thought. She began confidently. "I wondered if you'd tell me about what happened that day," she said, "when my father was killed and the money was lost."

There was an unexpected brusqueness in his voice as he an-

swered: "Your mother must have told you. She knows everything I know."

"But you were in the bank when—"

"Yes, I was in the bank. But I don't know what happened.
Nobody seems to know what happened. And if you have any
idea that you can find out, I'd say let it alone. It's nothing for
children to mix into. And, definitely, I won't have any hand in
helping you try."

Where was the soft and amiable gentleman Georgia had felt
so sure she had found in Uncle Vince? His back was stiff, his
face was almost stern, his eyes were boring into her. He looked
like—a lawyer, that was it. She would hate to have him
against her in court.

Then suddenly, he smiled. "Let's talk about the weather,"
he said. "Or about your school. How do you like Chet Lindsay? We think he's a fine teacher. And he, too, was one of
your father's best friends."

CHAPTER II

LANE HOUSE

"And was that a shock," said Georgia half-aloud, as she undressed that night. She was indignant, really. "Your father was
my best friend," he had said. And yet he wouldn't lift a finger
to help clear his best friend's name. She would have to ask
Mums about some of the things. Maybe Mr. Lindsay would
know about some of the others. But no, Mr. Lindsay had not
been in Lane's Cove then. He had a job in New Jersey. There
must be somebody, though. She set her lips in that determined
line. She would do it alone, if nobody would help.

Then a sudden thought struck her, almost with the force of
a blow. Uncle Vince was a lawyer. Did he know something
that he did not want her to find out? Something that would
show that his best friend had really taken the money? She
went to bed with a troubled mind.

As the week went on, she tried to absorb herself in school
and the work Herb was doing in the living room. By Friday
the patching was done there, woodwork and plaster, and Herb
was on his last day. She had scarcely exchanged a word with
him, and was surprised to see how silent he could be. How
much he talked to her mother while she was in school she did

not know. Once she had come back unexpectedly after starting for school in the morning, to find him not working but leaning over the desk. He must have been looking for a will, but she knew that there were no papers there of any sort, to find. Of course there wasn't any will.

The living room was going to be lovely. They had opened the fireplace, and were hoping to find andirons in the little attic, which was stuffed to the door with all sorts of discarded things.

"Didn't they ever throw anything away?" She and Mums were standing just inside the door, hopefully pushing aside chairs with loose rungs, old tables with scarred tops, rusty bedsprings.

"Not much, from the evidence," answered her mother. "There ought to be andirons here somewhere. See if you can wriggle in between here. You're smaller than I am."

"I can stand on the table and look down," said Georgia, "if it will hold me."

She climbed up, testing the top before she dared put her weight on it.

"Oh, look, Mums," she said when she was balanced and peering into the further corner under the eaves. "See that cute little desk. Oh, I want that, in my room. I'm going over there, and look into it." She stepped down warily and edged her way along. "Mums, there are things in it," she said. "Whose was it?"

"I don't know that, daughter. Remember I only visited here. It never was my home. What sort of things are there?"

"Papers, just a few." Georgia laughed nervously. "Maybe the will Herb's hunting for. Shall I bring them out?"

"Yes, but they're probably only old bills and receipts, and

things like that. I'm sure there isn't any will, and never has
been. Herb's just daydreaming."

Georgia gathered a thin bundle of papers and pushed them
into a pocket of her skirt. "Someday I'll come after you, little
desk," she said with a pat as she left it. "Now it's andirons."

They found the andirons a few minutes later, old handmade
ones, with sprawling legs and flattened ring tops.

"Exactly what we want," said Mrs. Lane happily. "They'll
fit the old fireplace as if they were made for it."

"Probably they were," Georgia replied. "And now they're
going back home."

She lifted them one by one over the table she had stood on to
survey the place, and then wormed her way out to the door.
Downstairs they put them into the fireplace and stood back to
see the effect.

Herb was packing his tools to go home, but came over to
look. "Out of the attic?" he asked. "What else is up there?"

"Oh, everything," said Georgia. "Everything in the world."
She remembered the papers in her pocket, but there was no
need to tell Herb about those, now anyway. They would look
at them when he had gone.

He was going now. "Nothing left to do but paint and paper,"
he said. "Might be some old paper like this left upstairs somewhere, so you wouldn't have to do it all over. Want me to
hunt?"

"I found some," answered Mrs. Lane, "in a box in the porch
chamber, and I brought it down. But this has faded so I don't
think we can use the new. I don't really like it very well anyway. We'll try to buy some, I think, and we'll put it on ourselves. Thanks for what you've done, Herb. Later, when I
can, I'd like to do more. But we have to stop now."

Georgia leaned over to set the andirons more symmetrically on the hearth, and the little packet of papers fell to the floor.

"What's that?" said Herb suspiciously. "Find something up there you wasn't going to let me know about?" He held out his hand.

Georgia had a fleeting fear. Suppose there was a will! And suppose they had to give up the house. She knew then that already she loved it, that for the first time in her life the place where she lived was more than a shelter, more than a roof. The new window, the spacious living room were hers. She could never face giving them up.

"We'll all look at the papers together, Herb," said Mrs. Lane quietly. "We just found them in the attic. From their look I'd guess they'd been there a long time. Aunt Susan's will was made only five years ago, after Uncle Joshua died."

She took the papers from Georgia, and slipped off the string that held them together. When the papers were spread on the kitchen table, Georgia wanted to laugh. An old, old deed, made when the first Burnham to live on Hackmatack had bought the place from one Lemuel Driscoll. A fire insurance policy, dated 1879. A small folder advertising kitchen pumps, and a folded page from the Kennebec *Journal,* filled with cooking recipes and "hints for housewives," with a date twenty years old.

Herb looked disappointed, but showed no real discomfiture. "It'll turn up," he said, and went back to putting planes and saws into his tool case. Then lifting it by its stout handle he started for the back door. "I don't really wish you any bad luck, Suze," he said. "But I still think the house orter be mine. I'm a generation near'n you are. It wouldn't be any more'n right."

There was no answer to that, and Herb left in his old car, that looked as if it would drop apart any minute but never did.

It was the middle of the next week before Georgia got an answer to the letter she had written Lorraine. The answer was a long one. Lorraine had seen Mrs. Allerton several times, and once had coaxed her to take a little walk in the evening. Georgia read:

"She really went. I didn't believe she would till we were outside the door, and even then I thought it was all off when the Carminello kids came swooping down on us, playing cops and robbers the way Tony and Luigi and their gang used to. If you're a Carminello you do play cops and robbers, no matter what year it is, I guess.

"Mrs. Allerton drew back and looked at them as if they were typhus germs or something, but they went by and she got a sort of second wind and we went on. She used to look at the sunsets over the Basin the way we do, she said, but she never had seen the lagoon with all the kids swimming, or the Shell. There was no Esplanade Concert that night, of course, because they don't start until July, but we walked around the Shell before she said we had to go in.

" 'I've heard the music faintly at home,' she said, 'and of course I've read about the concerts in the paper. But I never thought I'd like to come out, in the crowd. I do see now that it would be pleasant entertainment for a summer evening.'

"I don't know just when I'm going to say she ought to go to Maine for the summer the way she used to, and get away from everything here. But I shall do it someday, and then maybe some other day I'll begin to talk about Hackmatack Point.

"I think that's a super-special name, Hackmatack. And I just can't wait to see everything. School closes in three more weeks. Seems a long time, but perhaps it isn't too long to work on Mrs. Allerton. If I don't get her to Hackmatack I'll have to take a course in how to influence people. But I hope to do it without that.

"My mother doesn't see why I care. After all, it's Mrs. Allerton's business what she does. But Dad says, 'Go to it. It's time she was out—on parole, anyway.'"

Work on the new living room went fast, repainting woodwork and the old floor of wide pine boards, and putting on the new paper.

"I never knew you could do things like this," Georgia said to her mother, as they stood off to admire the wall they had finished the afternoon before. The new paper was lighter and warmer in tone than the old, and gave the whole room a different look. "I can't wait to see it done," Georgia continued. "I'd love to spend my life planning things like this."

"Perhaps you will. Who knows? We must be thinking about the parlor next. That won't be so much work, mostly arranging. I think there's a fireplace there too, but we won't do anything to it now."

"Not so much work," said Georgia, "but we have to get it done. Lorrie says—" and she launched into a report of the letter.

The days were growing longer now, and though mornings and nights were still cool, sunny days brought real warmth to the air. The big maple was dropping keys into the grass, the hackmatacks had tips of pale green growth on the ends of twigs and branches and little waxy rose-colored cones like jewels along the stems.

"Why, they're beautiful," said Georgia as Vee stopped the car one day beside a whole row of young trees beside the road. "If the cones just didn't have to get hard and brown."

"Well, they have to grow up, if that's what you mean. Guess everything has to do that, even us." And Vee grinned companionably. There was less argument between the two nowadays, the only subject they really disagreed about being what Vee still called "chasing crime."

Today, as Vee started the car again, Georgia brought up that subject again, ending mournfully with, "I don't know a bit more about it than I did when I came."

"Didn't expect you would," Vee returned. "Don't see how you think you could, when people like my dad gave it up. Dad's keen, you know."

"Vee," said Georgia hesitatingly, "I think your dad knows more than he wants me to find out. He was warning me off that night. But I have to know."

"All right," said Vee. "You have to know. But what do you do about it? Not a thing but talk, and talk doesn't solve mysteries. I'd either give up and say it doesn't matter, or I'd get busy on my own and stop thinking somebody would hand me what I want to know on a platter."

"I want to get busy and find out, but nobody will help me, even you."

"Nobody helped Columbus, at least not much, nor Galileo, nor any of the ones like that," said Vee.

"People might answer questions," protested Georgia, "but they won't, and Alice Soames is dead."

"Ask her sister, then. She's alive." Vee sounded the horn.

"Where?" asked Georgia eagerly.

"She's caretaker at the Lane House in the village. The Historical Committee hired her," explained Vee.

"You mean where we used to live?"

"Yes. She lives there all alone. Go and see her."

"I will. I'll go now. I'll walk to town," said Georgia.

"I'll take you," said Vee, backing the car into his own driveway, which they were passing, and turning back toward the village. "But I won't ask any questions. I'm no sleuth."

Several times in the weeks they had been at Hackmatack Georgia had thought of at least walking past the big old Lane house. It stood a little way from the center of the village, on a side street, sitting back behind a very ornamental white fence in front of a high lilac hedge.

"Like the sleeping beauty's palace," said Georgia as Vee brought the car to a stop. "You can hardly see the house at all."

"Annie's the sleeping beauty then," said Vee. "Go to the side door, and knock, pretty loud. She might be asleep, at that. She's getting old now."

"You know her," said Georgia. "Will she know me? I mean know who I am?"

"Oh, sure. Everybody knows the Lanes. And the Lane House, these days, makes even strangers know about the family. Probably ask Annie all sorts of questions."

"What do you mean? What about the Lane House?"

"Don't you know it's a show place? Open to the public in the summer, written about in magazines, finest wing staircase in New England, and all that? Why don't you know?"

"Mums never talks about it. She never talked about Lane's

Cove at all. I think she's glad it's a Burnham house we have now, and she'd like to forget she ever lived in that house, as a Lane. People must have been cruel to her."

"They were, probably," said Vee. "People can be. They don't use any sense about it, either."

Georgia stood on the side porch waiting an answer to her knock, and wondering what she should say when the door should open. What would Annie Soames be like? She heard footsteps inside and the door did open, slowly. Annie Soames was elderly, white-haired, but very straight and tall. She had no welcoming smile.

"Well?" she said, and waited.

Georgia for a second wished she had not come. But she was here, and she must say something.

"I am Georgia Lane," she began. "I was born in this house. May I come in?"

"Did you want something?" Annie Soames looked straighter and taller than ever. She made no move to open the door any further, but Georgia had a quick thought of Lorraine, "Getting a foot in the door." Georgia must do as well.

"Yes," she said. "I've been trying to remember. And I thought maybe you'd let me look. I lived here till I was six years old."

"Yes," said Annie. "I know." She still stood blocking the doorway. "I don't show the house."

"I'd like to talk to you," Georgia said. "You knew my father, and you must have known my mother too. We've come back to Lane's Cove. Please let me come in."

Annie Soames opened the door, but there was still no welcome in her face. "Your father killed my sister," she said, "killed her same as if he had stuck a knife in her heart. He took

"George was killed today," Georgia read in the diary.

that money, and worried her into her grave. She was never the same after that day."

She led the way into a room where she had evidently been sitting. Her knitting lay in a chair, the ball of yarn fallen on the floor beside it. She pointed to a chair, and Georgia dropped into it.

"Are you sure?" Georgia said. "Will you tell me what you know about that day?"

"I don't know a thing, myself," said Annie Soames. "I only know what my sister told me, and what I read after she died, in the diary she kept. That's all anybody knows." She picked up a worn leather-covered book from the table beside her chair.

"Oh, may I see it?" said Georgia. "May I?"

"Not to take away," said Annie. But she opened the book and said, pointing, "That was the day."

Georgia took the book in her hands. "What happened before that day?" she asked. "The day before, and other days?"

"Nothing," said Annie. "Turn back and you can see."

Georgia read the entries for several days. They were short and dull. The weather, always the weather. "Fair today," or "overcast" or "northeaster." Things like that. Then there were more things, about the bank, dull too. "Checked balance. O.K." or sometimes, "Five dollars short" or "$7.85 too much," but always followed by "Found error."

Until the day of the accident and the loss. That one began abruptly:

"George was killed today. It was just before three o'clock, and when he went out he said he'd be back in half an hour.

"I had just finished checking the cash and had laid aside

much more than usual for him to put into the safe. There was ten thousand dollars. He lifted the package of bills I had laid inside his desk and we talked about it. He said he was in a hurry, so he wouldn't do it till he came back. He would put it where it would be safe. I watched him put it under some folders in a drawer, and then I went back to the books.

"He had been gone only a minute, it seemed, when I heard the crash and saw people running down the hill to Cove Bridge. Tom was home sick and the only one around was Vince Allen, in the little Directors' Room in back. I was terribly excited, wondering what had happened, and when Vince ran out and down the hill I almost went, too, but then I remembered that I mustn't.

"I went outside, though, and stood there till somebody told me George was dead. A while after that, Vince came in to tell me to take care of the money and lock the bank. I went to George's desk. The ten thousand dollars wasn't there.

"Vince couldn't have taken it. He wasn't near where it was. But George could have. And now George was dead. Vince went back to see if the money was there, where the car had gone into the Cove, and then went to the house to see if it was in George's pocket or the brief case he had had in the car. There was nothing in either one.

"George might have taken it with him so he could know it was safe. Nobody seems to know where he was going when he went out, but everybody is wondering. Herb Small says he probably was going away somewhere and didn't mean to come back at all. But I don't think people would believe that. They would think he had the money and that when the car crashed and went into the Cove, the money somehow got washed away. It was just after flood tide and the current under the bridge is always terribly strong. That might have happened.

"I must try to make people think it was that way. I don't want them to think George was bad. That would be hard for Susie and little George. *They must think it happened the way I have said.*"

That was the last entry in the book. Georgia let the book close and laid it on the table. "Why isn't there any more?" she said at last.

"She would never write in it after that," said Annie. "She always tried to make people think George was all right, but if she had really thought so, she wouldn't have been the way she was." She looked at Georgia in a definitely hostile way. "I know he was your father," she said, "but I know too that there was something fishy about that story Alice kept telling folks. You could see, I could anyway, that she didn't believe it. And I never believed it, for a second."

"Who knew that he ever took the money with him at all?" asked Georgia coldly.

"Alice knew. She knew all the time, even when she said she couldn't remember. I am sure she knew. He put it in his pocket, and took it away with him."

"Ten thousand dollars, in his pocket?" Georgia's tone was scornful.

"It was in big bills. The Passapumset Paper Company had paid a loan that day. It was going to Bangor in the morning. Alice told me that."

"I don't believe any of it," said Georgia, flatly.

"Plenty of people do believe it, that he had it, I mean. And most of them think he had it for no good purpose. Probably he'd been playing poker with that worthless crowd down at Neal's, and got in debt. Or some other thing he shouldn't have been doing." A fierce light of conviction was in her eyes.

Georgia knew there was no use in trying to change her mind. But she said, "My father wasn't that kind of man."

"How do you know what kind of man he was? You were only a little young one then. He did it, he meant to do it, and it killed my sister. She went to pieces from that day."

Georgia rose swiftly from her chair. "Here's the book," she said. "Some way I'll find out what really happened. I'm going now."

It couldn't be like that, she thought wildly, as she went to the car where Vee was waiting. "I don't believe it. I don't believe it. I won't stop till I do find out."

CHAPTER 12

MORE CHANGES

Georgia wondered which way she should turn to find out more of what happened that day ten years ago. So far, she had discovered nothing at all except that her father had received the money from Alice Soames and had put it into his desk. After that he was responsible for it, and no one else had been near. Who else was there to ask?

"What are you thinking about, little George?" asked Vee as they bounced along on the road between the Corners and the Allen place. "You haven't told me yet what happened, or what you thought of Annie. How was she, cool like a cucumber, or raging like a lion?"

Georgia turned accusing eyes upon him. "You knew," she said, "how she would talk to me, and yet you told me to go."

"No," said Vee, with his wide-open smile. "I didn't know, I only guessed. Everybody knows how she feels about the whole thing, but then she would. She's always been a queer duck and she was kind of a care to Alice."

"Care? How?"

"Well, Alice really supported them, after their father was gone and Alice was old enough to have a job. I've heard Dad tell about it. They're sort of cousins of Dad's, you know.

Annie had a job once, in Tillie Wheelwright's store, tending the ice cream and pop counter. But Tillie said she scared all the kids away, so she lost the job and went back to being the housekeeper at home while Alice brought in the money."

"How did she get the job she has now? And what does she do there anyway?"

"Well, you see," said Vee, "she didn't have much to live on after Alice was gone. There had to be some way to take care of her. And about that time a big museum got its eye on the Lane house, and some of the smart women in town, Ma and some others, clubbed together, formed the Historical Committee, and the Committee bought it, so it would be preserved here. Somebody had to live in it, to keep it in shape, and they didn't want a family. So Annie got the job." He laughed. "No, I didn't mean that. So Annie was pushed into the job, fighting all the way."

Georgia was still full of questions. "What did they buy it for?" she asked next.

"Oh, it's a specimen, stuck up there with a pin through it, the way I used to fix butterflies. You don't appreciate what a fine house you picked out to be born in. And your mother sold it with everything in it, some of the things from way back around 1800. Guess all she wanted was to get away."

"And to get money for the bank," said Georgia. "But Annie said, 'I don't show the house.' What do they have it for then?"

"She doesn't show it. She'd scare people away, same as she did the kids in the store. She just keeps it clean and in order. They have somebody to take visitors around, but only in the summer. That's when folks are passing through and stop to see the wing staircase, the handmade beaded moldings, and all the rest. The house has got to be kind of famous."

"I don't really remember the house at all," said Georgia. "Just the lilacs. And all I remember of them is the smell."

"The lilacs have grown into a forest these days," said Vee. "They weren't like that when I was small. I'd have them cut back if I had the say. Ma thinks that, too. Maybe the Committee will."

They rode along, past the Allen place, and down the road till the low gray house under the big maple came in sight.

"This house must seem tiny to Mums, after living in a great specimen stuck through with a pin," said Georgia.

"Oh, it wasn't that then," said Vee. "It was just the biggest and finest house in town, and there were some others almost as good. But the others haven't been kept up, and they aren't much now."

So she had been born in the biggest and finest house in town, Georgia thought. And then had gone to live in what Mums called "a room and a half" in a crowded city.

Vee was still talking. She began to listen again. "We're all proud of the Lane House," he said. "Wait till summer, and see the road signs. 'Five miles—or ten miles—to the Lane House, home of one family for 150 years. Wing staircase, famed "thousand carvings," many of the original furnishings.' "

"You sound like a sideshow man at the circus." Georgia turned to laugh at him.

"Well, the Lane House helps to put Lane's Cove on the map."

"I like *this* house," said Georgia as they came opposite the big tree, "I like it more every day."

"Fine," said Vee. "Maybe you'll even like the country after a while."

"Maybe," said Georgia, but she knew that she had begun to like it now.

The new living room was finished, and with the old furniture and softly tinted curtains, the opened fireplace, the added sun pouring in through the extra window on the west, it was "just exactly the way I wanted it," Georgia said.

The bedroom was in order now, too. "It will be cold in winter, with those north windows," Mrs. Lane said regretfully, "but we needn't use it then. There is plenty of room upstairs."

Georgia gave a last pat to the old bedspread of handmade sheeting studded all over with hobnail tufts of candlewick, all white, and ruffled to the floor. "I never thought we were coming to things like this," she said. "When I first saw the house it looked to me like nothing but a gray old shell. I know now that there were treasures inside."

"Treasures outside, too," said her mother. "Wait till you see midsummer on Hackmatack."

"Lorrie and I will see it together. In two weeks she will be here." Then Georgia laughed. "Wonder how she is doing, influencing people, meaning Mrs. Allerton. Wouldn't you be surprised if Mrs. Allerton should want to come?"

"I'm afraid I should. By now, though, I wish she would. A little money would be a help, and I don't quite dare try to get anyone else until Lorraine has had her chance. She would never forgive me."

They closed the door on the parlor bedroom, as Georgia still called it, and went out to supper in the kitchen.

"Now," said Georgia coolly, "I can begin thinking about turning that little room back of this into a kitchen and making this lovely place into a dining room and my study."

"This lovely place?" said Mrs. Lane. "This not the kitchen any more? Aunt Susan would rise up—"

"Aunt Susan said make it into a home. And this is a lovely

place. Sun from the east in the morning, sun from the west in the afternoon. Light from both sides all day long. It deserves better than dirty dishes in the sink and an old stove covered with pots and pans."

Mrs. Lane had to admit that dirty dishes, pots and pans did nothing for the room. In fact she remembered that the little room at the back had been "the sink room" when she first came to visit the house.

"They changed it when they were getting old and wanted things easier, I think," she said.

"Well, we aren't old and we want things right instead of easy," said Georgia.

Her mother laughed. "You sound like sixteen," she said. "What is any obstacle but something to hurl yourself at? We might move the sink," she conceded. "I'll think about it."

"It's as good as gone," said Georgia. "And after that—"

Mrs. Lane put up her hands in protest. "Let's stop there, for a while. I'd like to get my breath."

It was the day after that that Georgia came home from school to find Liza sitting with her mother in the kitchen, having a companionable cup of tea. The car Georgia had seen Herb drive stood in the driveway, but Herb was nowhere to be seen.

"Did you drive yourself?" Georgia asked, after greetings had been exchanged.

"Yes," said Liza, with her soft comfortable drawl. "Wonder how we ever got along without the car. We're just too far from the village for lazy folks like me to walk, and besides, I keep getting hurry calls on the telephone to go where there's sickness."

"Nursing?" said Mrs. Lane. "I didn't know you did that."

"Yes," said Liza. "There isn't any regular nurse in town any more, so I go in to do for folks when they need me. The longest spell I ever had on one case was when Alice Soames was sick and died. I was there weeks and weeks."

Georgia, who had been only half listening, sat up straighter at that. She must ask Liza about Alice. Mums still couldn't bear to talk about anything connected with that awful time. Georgia could see that, and she knew now why she herself had known so little about Lane's Cove, the beautiful old Lane house, and all the rest. When they had gone away, Mums had meant never to go back, and to put all that part of her life behind her. She had thought Georgia need never know about it, either. But things hadn't worked out that way. Mums had pretended, there in Boston, that everybody would have forgotten, but she knew they would not.

"I must plan how I can see Liza, alone, and find out whether Alice, in those last days, talked about what had happened. That's important," she thought. "But maybe Liza'll tell me more if she doesn't realize how much I want to know." She began to make a plan.

School was coming nearer to the end. When Lorraine had written that she had two more weeks, Lane's Cove High School had only one. Junior Talent Night came, and Georgia, having no part in the program, had been impressed into service as ticket taker at the door, and had seen some curious looks directed her way. "George Lane's kid," she felt they were thinking. She was sure that everybody knew who she was.

Mona, who was to sing and whose high, birdlike voice Georgia had heard in morning assembly, came by, in pale blue ruffled taffeta, looking tinier than ever in the long billowing skirt, and with her face turned away as if Georgia were not there. Most of the performers had come in the back door, but not Mona. And to Georgia's astonishment, just behind Mona, apparently with her, came Curt.

It really was funny to see Curt carrying over his arm the long evening cape Mona had taken off the moment she crossed the threshold, and had pushed into his reluctant hands. On his face was a combination of fear, resentment, and yes, Georgia was sure she saw pride. It was probably the first time he had ever taken a girl anywhere, she decided.

"Bet she made him," said a voice at her elbow, and there was Vee. "Good thing, though. Exactly what the doctor'd order for a guy like Curt. Wonder how she cracked his shell."

Mona and Curt disappeared through the door that led to the stage but a short time later Curt came back alone and stood there where Georgia was mechanically reaching out her hand for tickets while she listened to Vee's whispered comments on the people coming in.

"Gee," Curt muttered, "hot around here." And he tried to loosen his collar until Vee said urgently: "Hey, don't do that. You'll ruin your whole getup." And Georgia added, "You don't know how fine you look, Curt."

"Didn't want to come at all," said Curt a little sulkily, and Vee shot a triumphant look at Georgia, behind Curt's back.

The end of the school year came nearer. Now finals were over, unfortunates who had flunked courses knew it, attendance at school was perfunctory that last week. Seniors who had parts for Class Day and Commencement—graduation, they called it here—might be heard at all sorts of odd times rehearsing in Study Hall, with a little knot of teachers as audience, and everybody else shut out.

Vee would be valedictorian. Of course he would, Georgia

thought. Vee would always be near the top, whatever he under-took, though she knew he would have stiff competition when he went away to encounter top students from the best schools of the country. Those schools could give more than a little school like this could ever hope to do, but Vee was the kind to take a handicap as a challenge.

Look at the way he worked over his railroad hobby. It seemed to her that he had facts about the history and develop-ment of the various roads of the country oozing from his finger-tips. He was writing about these things for the essay that would precede his brief valedictory address. "Transportation as a Major Industry." The subject sounded dull to Georgia, but she knew Vee wouldn't sound dull to his audience, no matter what he said. He was that kind.

Early that week Georgia had a letter from Lorraine. It said:

"Only one week after this. Then I'll be a full-fledged senior. And so will you.

"Now hold your breath! Mrs. Allerton asked me what part of Maine you were in, and was it right on the sea. And was I going to visit, or would I be a boarder. 'A boarder,' I said firmly, but I did admit that I'd be a visiting boarder at that. Then I said you had room for more people, and that I was sure your mother would like to have some-body, somebody nice, I said. She needed to have the house make some money for her, I thought.

"Then, innocent as a lamb, 'Why don't you go down there with me? And get away from Kendall Street for all summer. It must be a lovely place.' I talked right along, about how I liked the name Hackmatack Point, and Ar-rowhead Bay, too. She brightened up and said hackmatacks were beautiful trees, so delicate and feathery. I said I couldn't wait to see them, but I didn't say any more about her going. I thought I'd better let the idea sink in.

"You tell your mother to decide how much she wants to charge for 'a nice boarder,' and I'll have the price on the end of my tongue when Mrs. Allerton asks me. She will. I know she will."

Georgia finished reading the letter to her mother, and they both went in to look once more at the parlor bedroom. The starched white lace curtains, with their big roses, had been replaced by the filmy marquisette ones they had had in Kendall Street. They hung now at the four windows, pushed back almost to the window frames, so that the green outdoors was all there, in plain sight.

The bed had been an ugly metal one. No "Early American" there. But probably Aunt Susan had thought it was wonderful when she had bought it to replace some old four-poster. Mums had decided that they would have to use it and it was Mums who had used the hacksaw herself to make it look as it did now.

The high old headboard with its open metal scrolls was gone, and the low and not too bad footboard had taken its place by simply turning the bed around. And now there was no footboard at all. The lovely hobnailed coverlet hung all around without a break, and the bed looked like a beautifully cut white mound of snowflakes, Georgia thought.

The bureau was old pine, from which she had helped her mother take several layers of different colored paint, and which now had the dull satiny finish that Mums had somehow known how to get with repeated applications of oil.

There was a little old rocking chair, pine too, and obviously handmade. That had come from the attic, with the seat all gone, but now it had a seat and a cushion they had made from the scanty remains of a thin old hooked rug. There had been nothing left except the center, but it had made a wonderful cushion, its bunch of faded flowers coming right in the middle. "It looks as if it had meant to be a cushion all the time," Georgia had said.

She was certain that Mrs. Allerton would come. "Lorrie'll do it," she had said when she had finished reading the letter, and they both laughed at Lorraine's cheerful certainty.

Mrs. Lane had said, "We'd better set a price and let her know, or she'll be sending a telegram or something, to find out." She smoothed a tiny wrinkle from the hobnailed spread, and plumped one of the pillows under it, using the flat of her hand to push the spread tight so that the pillows made one continuous straight line.

They closed the door on the parlor bedroom, and Georgia went at once to answer Lorraine's letter. "How much, Mums?" she called from the desk in the living room, and together they decided what they should ask.

"It will be really wonderful if she comes," Mrs. Lane said. "Just that much more would make me feel safe."

"She'll come," said Georgia. "I'll bet on Lorrie. Now I'll finish the letter. And as soon as school is really closed, we can begin fixing the new kitchen. Nice and modern—well, as modern as we can, with nothing but the old things to put in it. But we'll arrange it 'with a maximum of efficiency,' as Miss Clark at the interior decorating class used to say. She was strong on kitchens. And I'm going to be too."

CHAPTER 13

AFTERNOON WALK

"Well, that's over," said Georgia the morning after the graduating exercises had formally closed the school year.

Like all the other newly made seniors, she had been an usher at the exercises, and though she had not had a new dress for the occasion, her candy-striped taffeta was new to Lane's Cove and she knew it was pretty and becoming. So she had not minded when Mona and her crowd had stared and commented to each other as she joined the other ushers receiving instructions about their duties.

She had thought Curt looked a little more easy in his dress-up clothes this time, and she smiled as she noticed that he was keeping away from Mona and her friends. His being there among the ushers showed that in spite of his French he had made his promotion and was now a senior like the rest. She was glad of that.

When they went to their posts, it happened that Georgia and Curt were assigned to the same aisle, and she saw him clutching tickets from people with frantic energy and to some extent forgetting himself as he put his mind on matching reserved ticket stubs with the seats they represented. But she had not long to watch him. The crowd seemed to come all at once, and she was busy herself, but she had seen enough to be sure that Curt had taken another step toward emerging from his shell.

Once she saw him in argument with Herb Small, who had no patience, it seemed, with the "folderol" of having any reserved seats at a graduation.

" 'Twasn't so in my day," Herb said loudly. "First come, first served. All have equal chance at paying taxes, don't we? School belongs to taxpayers. Ought to have equal chance at getting the front seats."

Curt seemed to be trying to explain, but Herb interrupted with: "What's that? Seats saved for folks that have somebody graduating? I say they ain't got any rights I ain't got." But Liza pulled him into line and they subsided into seats back of the dividing line between reserved and unreserved.

The hall was crowded. Everybody in town must come to graduation, Georgia thought, and she could see the need of reserved places for the families of the graduates. Otherwise they might not have got in at all.

Now it was the first day of vacation, and she ate her breakfast slowly, without even glancing at the clock. The door between kitchen and living room was open, and the early June sun filtering in through the maple leaves to the eastern windows made wavering lights and shadows on Aunt Susan's old hand-hooked rugs on the living-room floor. The kitchen windows on that side were a little more shadowed by the tree, but she could look out to bright sun on the grass, and clear blue sky above.

Hackmatack in summer was going to be beautiful, as Mums had said. And Georgia realized suddenly that she knew noth-

ing at all about summer outside the city. She had seen the sun
glitter on the Charles River Basin, and a few times from some
excursion beach on open water, but never anything like Arrowhead Bay. It must be a mile or two across to the next point,
which stretched along parallel to Hackmatack and was fringed
with dark green behind the water. If she had a boat, and could
row, she would row across and see at close quarters what was
on that other point. Probably the Allens had a rowboat. Perhaps Vee would take her out someday.

Her thoughts shifted. If Mrs. Allerton came, the money she
paid would keep Mums from worrying, and the question of
finding some way to earn money for the future could be put
off for a while. There were just two things that Georgia herself had laid out in her mind to get done before the summer
was over. One, of course, was to keep on trying to clear her
father's name in the bank loss, and the other to study out ways
to make the old house pleasanter and more comfortable without spending much money.

She knew that almost anyone would say she was too young
to accomplish either of these things. Too young even to plan
remodeling a house. But if she intended to make that sort of
thing her work, to earn her living that way someday, it would
do no harm to be thinking about it now.

Vee had told her about the State Library in Augusta, from
which books might be obtained at no cost except for postage.
That was the way he got most of his railroad books, and he was
sure that books about houses and furnishings could be found
there too. She would write and ask today.

She rose from the table and set about washing her own and
her mother's breakfast dishes. Mums was already at work in
the garden, which was to have a large part in feeding them

through the summer. The stores on the hanging shelves in the cellar would be waiting after frost had come. Mums liked to work in gardens, but Georgia was not sure that she would like it at all. However, she must try to help. Mums mustn't do it alone.

As she put her hands into the foamy hot dishwater, which felt good even on a June morning, on Hackmatack, she took up the problem of getting to see Liza, alone. Vee would take her, she was sure, but she really would prefer to go by herself, and to say nothing about it either. She could walk, easily enough, and once at the center of the village, it wasn't far after that. She would find some errand to take her to the village, this afternoon. Perhaps they would need something at the store.

She put away the last of the few dishes, and rinsed the dish towels, hanging them outdoors on the back-yard clothesline. Now she would help in the garden for a while, take care of her room, and then she could be free for the afternoon.

"Hi, Mums," she said as she came to the edge of the small garden, where her mother was busy weeding a row of tiny lettuce plants. "What can a greenhorn do?"

"Plenty," said Mrs. Lane, "if you really want to help."

"Okay," said Georgia. "What do I do?"

They weeded together companionably for a while, then as the sun mounted higher and began to beat down on them, they went into the house.

"I do like it here, Mums," said Georgia a little shamefacedly, "even if I did make a fuss about coming. I'm even glad we don't live right in the village. I wouldn't have believed that of myself before we came."

"I like it here on the Point," said her mother. "But you won't be lonesome out here now that school is over, will you, Georgia?"

"If I am, there are places to go. Besides, you forget. Lorrie'll be here in a week and I'd defy anybody to be lonesome where she is."

"Of course," and her mother laughed. "One day less than a week, at that. You'll probably get a letter today telling what train to meet."

"And whether she's alone or not," Georgia replied.

Mrs. Lane laughed. Then she grew suddenly serious. "There's one thing," she said, and hesitated a little before going on. "About—"

"You mean the bank affair," said Georgia bluntly. "I've been thinking about that. Mrs. Allerton, if she comes, might not hear about it, but Lorrie's sure to, somewhere. Lorrie always hears about everything. She's that kind. There'll be Herb, if he comes to move the sink and the stove. He'd love to tell her all about it, and then about the will that's going to let him take the house away from us. We'd better tell her ourselves, then anything he says won't matter." She had a quick thought. "Have you spoken to Herb about the kitchen job?"

"Not yet," her mother replied. "But I suppose if he could come it might be better to do it this week, while we're still alone. Sometime when Vee or Mart is driving to the village—"

"We don't have to ask them, Mums. I can walk. I'd like to. And we don't want to keep asking them all the time, do we?"

"No, I don't like to be a nuisance. They've been so kind."

"Okay. This afternoon I'll set out, and I'll come back with Herb roped, tied and thrown. You can guess what I've been reading. Vee lends them to me."

It was still early in the afternoon when Georgia did set out for the village. She was annoyed when she had passed the Fairchild lane to see Mona only about a hundred feet ahead of her, also apparently walking to the village. That meant keeping the pace Mona set, or going even more slowly than that. She had no intention of catching up to Mona. So all the way to the Corners she walked along behind, and, ignoring Mona, tried to put her mind on the problem of getting Liza to talk and of what questions she would need to ask.

Turning right at the Corners, before long they would pass the Kennedy farm, with the most businesslike equipment and the widest fields and pastures of any place she had seen around Lane's Cove. Perhaps Curt would be in sight somewhere and she could stop to talk until Mona got out of sight ahead. Unless Mona had the same idea. In that case it would be Georgia who would hurry by and set the pace herself.

It was ridiculous, she thought, for people to act as she and Mona were doing, but after all, it was Mona who had set the pace there, too. Who would want to be friends with anybody like that? Nobody, she thought triumphantly.

She looked ahead, beyond Mona, toward the Kennedy place on the left. There was Curt, in overalls and no shirt, on his knees weeding a long row of beans almost beside the road.

Mona did stop, and she could see Curt lift his head, say "Hi," then doggedly return to his weeding, while Mona carried on a sprightly conversation, with what help she could extract from Curt in the way of nods and an occasional *Yes* or *No*.

Georgia was close to them now, and meant to get by without even calling a greeting, but Curt saw her and she couldn't quite pass him without a word. But she did not slow her pace, until he said, "What's your hurry?" and then flatly, "Good-by, Mona."

Georgia gasped at that, and at the swift way Mona turned and went on up the road.

Curt grinned, the first time Georgia could remember seeing anything but an anxious look on his face. "Sorry," he said. "But I had to get rid of her somehow. She pesters me."

"I'll stay till she gets out of sight," Georgia returned. "Then I won't have to look at her back all the way to town."

"Somebody'll give you a lift," said Curt, and went back to his weeding.

"I don't mind walking," said Georgia. "I'm really going beyond the village. Over to Herb Small's. He's going to do some work for us."

"Funny bird, Herb." Georgia became conscious that for the first time since she had known him Curt was talking, of his own accord. "Handles his tools all right, though," he said.

This was animated conversation for Curt, and Georgia lingered a minute more to encourage him, then said she must go on.

"Walking back, too?" he asked. Then, with a reckless plunge: "I'm driving up later, come back around five. Bring you back, if you say."

Georgia accepted at once. It would never do to refuse, she knew. The crack in Curt's shell would close up again tight at a rebuff. Besides, she would rather ride than walk. One way was enough.

"I'll meet you at the post office, then, at five," she said. "Now I'll have to go."

By the time she reached the Small place, she had decided to tell Liza exactly what she wanted and why, because there seemed no other way to account for all the questions she wanted to ask. But Herb must not be there, and she hoped he would be working outdoors, or perhaps be away on a job. She looked for signs that Liza was in the house.

The side door was open and, encouraged, she stepped up and knocked. But it was Herb's voice that shouted, "Come in," and there was no sign of Liza when she was inside.

"In here," Herb, still out of sight, continued. She found him in the front room, leaning back in the big easy chair with his feet on a stool, and with a mystery magazine in his hands.

"Are you sick?" she asked.

"Not exactly sick," he said, mildly indeed, for Herb. "Wasn't quite up to the mark this morning, so I been here all day. Have spells like that sometimes. Tired," he said solemnly. "No strength at all."

"I'm sorry," said Georgia. "We had a job for you."

"Tearing the place to pieces some more?" he said, and let go of the magazine, which fell to the floor with a clatter.

"Not tearing anything to pieces. Just moving things around," answered Georgia.

"What? Where?" Herb showed no lack of strength as he came to his feet and eyed her sharply. "Don't know but I ought to put an injunction on you people to stop your goings-on till it's settled whose house it really is."

"It is settled," said Georgia.

"Not if I find that other will," snapped Herb. Georgia wanted to laugh.

"How long are you going to keep on thinking about that?" she asked. "It's nearly two years since Aunt Susan died."

"*My* Aunt Susan," insistently. "Your mother's great-aunt, and your great-great. Pretty slim relation, I call it. She was my Marm's own sister, and I don't think she had any idea of letting the place go out of the family."

"What family?" Georgia was ready to argue it out with him this time. "That was a Burnham house. Burnhams had been there a long time before Aunt Susan married one and went there to live. And she left it to a Burnham, my mother. Now let's talk about work. We might agree better about that."

Herb sniffed angrily. "What about work?" he said.

"Well," said Georgia, "if you get your strength back, we thought you might come some day this week to move the sink, and maybe the stove, to the small room back of the kitchen. We'll have everything ready."

"I'll come," said Herb. "Keep an eye on you folks. Tear the house down if you get a chance."

That business concluded and the date set, Georgia said, "Where's Liza?"

"Liza? Case of sickness down the road. She'd ought to be along about now, though. She telephoned she'd be here to get my supper. Glad of that. Ain't got no strength at all today." He was back in the chair and reaching for the magazine as Georgia went out.

She was well on the road to town when she saw Liza coming toward her on the left side of the road.

"Been to my house?" Liza called as they approached each other. And when Georgia had answered, Liza came to a stop and said with a twinkle in her eye, "Herb got caught up on his reading yet?"

"She knows how to manage him," Georgia thought as they both laughed. And Georgia asked, "How is your patient?"

"Oh, not really a patient this time. Just being neighborly, go in to help out."

"What does Herb do when you go on a long case, like Alice Soames, for instance?"

"Oh," said Liza, with another twinkle, "Herb's all right about taking care of himself, when he has to. No man likes to fry his own potatoes or boil his own eggs, but Herb can. I don't like his messing up my pantry either, but we need the money, so we both make out."

"It must have been hard when you stayed so long at the Soames'."

"It was. Alice was sick a long time."

"Liza." Georgia took the plunge. "Did she ever talk about the bank—and the money?"

"Not much." Then Liza looked Georgia straight in the eye. "And I wouldn't tell you if she did. It's like a doctor. He don't tell."

Georgia hadn't thought of it that way. "But if she knew—"

"If she knew, she didn't tell me. I can say that much. She didn't talk much anyway. She just wrote in her diary, and what went in there wasn't any of my business."

"Annie said she never wrote in it after that day," Georgia said.

"Well, she never did, I guess, that one Annie sets such store by. But she had another one, that I suspect Annie never saw. Kept it under her pillow, night and day. Maybe she started it after she stopped writing in the other one. Folks that keep diaries get the habit pretty strong."

"What became of it?" asked Georgia.

"I wouldn't know. Toward the last she didn't have it 'round, but I don't know when it disappeared, or how. Maybe she threw it into the fire. She could have. And that's all I have to tell you, or anybody. And I'd better be getting along. Herb'll be getting hungry." She smiled but Georgia knew the subject was closed.

"Thanks," she said.

"I wouldn't dig in too deep into that old affair, if I was you," Liza said. "Those that haven't forgot it will soon. You'd better try to forget it too."

"Now what did she mean by that?" Georgia said aloud, as the distance widened between her and Liza. And she walked along rapidly, to keep her appointment with Curt at the post office at five.

CHAPTER 14

THE SUMMER CLUB

"Sure, I'm taking you down all the way," said Curt as they rode along between the village and the Corners. Then with an unusual burst of loquacity: "Ever see the pitcher plants that grow along the haith here? Not far from the road."

Haith bothered Georgia for a moment. Then she concluded that it probably meant heath, the way a fish weir in the bay was always called a *wair*. And the heath must be this level stretch of land with low-growing plants and thickets of alder that ran for a mile or two on both sides of the road.

Curt stopped the car, dashed through a swampy place where Georgia could hear the water squash and gurgle under his feet, and came back wet but triumphant with a handful of strange-looking plants.

These must be the pitcher plants, Georgia guessed, with their tubular leaves that did look like pitchers, thick and shaded from green to deep winecolor. In the other hand Curt held a single lady's slipper, rising from spreading leaves and nodding on a slender stem.

"See," he said. "Hundreds of them in there."

"Aren't these queer?" said Georgia, looking into the scalloped top of a pitcher. "And this one's lovely. I never saw anything like either of them before."

"Wouldn't, living in the city," answered Curt. He started the car again and Georgia, holding the plants carefully, thought that she and Curt were really getting on very well.

But her satisfaction was short-lived. Ahead of them as they came around a curve from the heath to the top of the hill that dipped to the head of the bay was Mona. And when they reached her Curt slowed up and came to a stop with, "Going down your way. Hop in."

Mona looked ready to refuse, but seemed to change her mind, and got into the back seat, slamming the door with a loud crack. After that there was no conversation. They turned at the Corners, and then in at the Fairchild lane, and when Curt stopped the car by the house, Mona got out and gave the door another slam.

"Thanks," she said, without a backward glance, and ran up the walk to the door.

"And that's that," said Curt.

"Why, he's getting positively talkative," Georgia thought. And then he surprised her even more.

"What's eating her anyhow?" he said. "Acts like a four-year-old. My colt Hurricane'd have better sense."

"She has a grudge against my father," said Georgia. "I'd give my soul to prove she's wrong."

"Yeah," said Curt thoughtfully. "Can see you would. Question is, how. All happened a long time ago."

"There must be some way," said Georgia. "I've just been talking to Liza Small. About Alice Soames."

"Who was she, Annie's sister that died? Annie's a queer one. What would the sister know?"

Curt came back with a handful of strange-looking plants.

Georgia sighed. "She might have known a lot. She worked in the bank, and she was the one who found out the money was gone. She kept a diary, but it disappeared. She might have thrown it into the stove, Liza said. I wish she hadn't, because that diary could maybe tell me what I want to know."

"Sure, it could, or then again it might not tell a thing. Maybe it didn't go into the stove. Maybe it's still there. In the house, I mean."

"What house? Annie doesn't live where they used to. She lives in the Lane House," Georgia said.

"Yeah, I know. Now let me think." And Georgia was obligingly silent. In a few minutes they reached the house and she was rising to get out. Curt seemed to be still thinking.

"Thanks, Curt," she said. "It was fine for you to bring me all the way down. Come in?"

Curt shook his head. "Chores to do," he said. "But I'll keep thinking. Might be some way."

Georgia wished as she entered the house that Vee could be interested the way Curt seemed to be, in proving that her father had not taken the money. Vee was really a thinker. Curt was probably slow-witted. Nobody who was very keen would muddle things the way he did in French class. His "thinking" wouldn't get very far, but it was good of him to want to help.

"Mail," called Mrs. Lane from upstairs when Georgia was inside the house. "On the desk. One for you from Lorraine, and I had one from Mrs. Allerton. I'll be down in a minute."

Georgia tore open Lorraine's letter. "She wants to come" was the opening sentence. "I walked up to North Station last night and got a timetable. We get to Lane's Cove at 5:55, and the smile that I'll have on when you see me will almost meet around the back of my head. Look for the smile and I'll be behind it. I can't wait for the day to come. Oh, did I say Monday? I don't believe I did. Monday, the twenty-first of June. I'll be seeing you."

Mrs. Lane came downstairs and handed Georgia the second letter to read. Mrs. Allerton had written:

"For the first time in many years I think it best to get away from the heat and noise of Kendall Street in summer. Your daughter's friend, Lorraine, has somehow broken down my defenses, and I can see now that I have been more than foolish to ignore the neighborhood I used to love and had grown to hate. People don't have to be like ourselves, I find, to have something to give us. I owe this to a young girl, or perhaps a little to myself, when I had that strange impulse to offer you beds for that last night before you went away.

"Lorraine says that you would take me into your home for a few weeks of the hot season, and she quoted terms you had given her 'for a nice boarder,' as she put it. I would try to be that, and if you will let me know that it is satisfactory to you, I will come with Lorraine on Monday, the twenty-first. I hope that this will meet with your approval and that I shall see you then. I spent all my girlhood summers at a farm on the coast of Maine, and I loved it."

"We don't have to worry about that any more," said Georgia. "Income assured. Aunt Susan's house pays its way. I mean *our* house, and I wish I could remember to say it that way. Our roof, our heads, our house!"

"Income assured sounds beautifully final," said her mother, "but really it is only a breathing space. Not that I want to be a pessimist, but there's college or art school, or whatever it is you need, and I want to be sure you get it when the time comes. So I still have to look for some kind of permanent income. But the breathing space comes now just at the right time."

"It arrives on Monday, the twenty-first. The room is ready, and Herb will fix the little kitchen. Come on, Mums. Let's go out there and clear out the boxes and barrels, so we can plan the new shelves and cupboards. I'm dying to be efficient."

"New shelves and cupboards? The camel again?"

"Well, there are some nice new boards in the barn, a whole pile of them. And Herb is handy with tools. Modern kitchens are all lined with those things, you know that, Mums." And Georgia smiled her most winning smile.

"To tell the truth, I was planning something of that sort myself," admitted her mother. "We might put our heads together."

They went happily out to what was to be the new kitchen, where they pushed and pulled, measured and planned, and hoped that it wouldn't take Herb too long to make the room what they wished.

The June evenings were near their greatest length. There were hours after supper before the light died out. Sometimes she and her mother watched the sunset, vivid and ever-changing in the west, but with reflected glory all around the circle of the sky. Sometimes they walked up to the Allens' and Georgia played darts with Vee and the children at the target board set up in the field next the house. More often they stayed at home, with Georgia curled up on the couch under the west windows in the living room with a book, and her mother sitting near, both where they could watch the bright sky on one side and the delicate tracery of maple leaves against the blue on the other.

They were there one night when Georgia heard a car drive into the yard, and the rise and fall of girls' voices. She went out, to greet Mag and Edwina, conscious of the fact that this was their first visit and that their coming gave her a warm feeling. She did want to belong. This was a step.

"Hi, George," they called, almost in unison. "Now school's over," added Edwina, "we have time to come calling. And Pop broke down and let me have the car."

"Have you a license?" asked Georgia.

"Oh, yes, but that doesn't count with Pop. He's sure I'll get off the road and pile up the car, not to mention ourselves, on the rocks somewhere."

"Oh, Eddie," said Mag, "we don't go within half a mile of the shore anywhere till we get right here. And we'd have to buck the birches here to get to it."

"That doesn't count with Pop either. He has a great imagination, my pop. Especially where his darling daughter is concerned. He's always wondering how I've lived to grow up this far, and he can picture me drowned and run over, both at the same time, any time I'm out of his sight."

"She's talking nonsense," said Mag. "But I guess you know that."

"Nice doorway," said Edwina, as they approached the front door. "I like the old sidelights. They don't seem to make them around here any more. Some of these little old houses have a lot of—what-do-you-call-it?—dignity, I guess."

"I love houses, inside and out," said Georgia. "Come in and see our new living room. I'm proud as a peacock over its fancy tail."

When Georgia had introduced them to Mrs. Lane, they admired the living room and even had a glimpse of the parlor bedroom. Then they settled down to talk. As the gay conversation went on, Georgia knew how she had missed having girls at her home, and why she longed so intensely for Lorraine to come. Vee had been fine, and had saved her many a lonesome hour, "but you need your own kind, too," she realized. It was wonderful to have Mag and Edwina come.

"We're beginning to think about the Summer Club," said Edwina after a while. "We have it every year. Too busy when there's school, so we start up as soon as vacation comes and run till school begins again. You have to join."

"Is it a big club?" asked Georgia. "And who belongs?"

"Big? In Lane's Cove?" Edwina laughed, while Mag explained: "Most of the girls our age. There are about twenty or thirty, I guess. We haven't counted up yet this year, but we will when we get together."

"We meet afternoons," said Edwina, "once a week. And we do something to raise money. Summer Club Show, we call it."

"What's the money for?" asked Georgia.

"Different things, different years. The Club decides, but it's something for the school most years. Last year we bought some stuff for the lab that Mr. Lindsay said we ought to have but that the town was too poor to buy."

Georgia hesitated a little before asking: "Is Mona in the Club? And those girls she manages?"

Edwina and Mag both laughed. "Manages is right," said Mag. "She makes them jump through hoops, like my puppy Sparks."

"Yes, she'll be there," said Edwina. "They all will. But she can't pull any of her tricks. We won't let her. Funny, we never noticed before this spring how poisonous she could be. Competition, I guess."

"That's it," said Mag. "She thought she had Vee hooked onto her little finger, with Curt there in the back of the car, to use if she wanted him. Then you came, and she found out Vee was a free man and would go where he liked. And that even Curt didn't like it much when she made him take her to Talent Night and carry the velvet cape."

Georgia had agreed to join the Club before she remembered that Lorraine would be here, but when she mentioned it the girls said that Lorraine should join also. "It's summer for her too, isn't it?" Edwina said. "You'll both like it. We have fun."

Georgia knew that Lorraine would like it, and she felt sure that Lane's Cove girls would like Lorraine. She was less sure of her own standing in the Club. Mona's crowd could make things all wrong for her and she doubted that her two friends could control Mona's undercover slurs and schemes. But she didn't dare refuse to join. That would shut her away from most of the summer fun that the other girls were set to enjoy. It would make her seem different, and she knew that in spite of everything she must seem like the rest and do the things they did.

Time went quickly as the three girls talked in the living room while Mrs. Lane sat at the big kitchen table writing letters. It was deep twilight before the two visitors noticed how late it was.

"Look, Eddie," said Mag suddenly, "we won't get back to the black road much before dark, now. And if we don't start, your pop'll have the constable out searching for you."

"He will, at that," said Edwina. "And we'll never get the car again. So long, George. Remember, Wednesday next week, at my house, two o'clock. Be there early, and bring Lorraine."

There was the sound of grinding gravel as the car started

and Georgia stood watching it up the road until only its tiny red light at the back could be seen. This was another step toward being part of the life of Lane's Cove, the life that she had thought once she had no desire to share.

At school they had had to accept her, or pretend to anyway. But now there was no necessity, and there was always Mona to stir up trouble if she could. Georgia had nothing with which to fight back, unless she could clear her father's name. Everything seemed to lead back to that. And leading back there, stopped short. She was no nearer a solution of the mystery than the day she and her mother had stepped off the train at the Lane's Cove station. What should she do?

She went in to the living room, where Mums was already lighting the lamp.

"It's almost bedtime," Mums said, "but we can read for a while. I get sleepy early when I work so much in the garden. I'm really a little sleepy now."

Georgia was not sleepy. There were too many problems crowding upon her. "Mums," she said abruptly, "I know you don't like to talk about it, but why should Alice Soames be so upset about that money if nobody blamed her?"

"Anybody would be upset about a loss of so much money as that. I don't think they ever did blame her, but she was our friend, and she tried so hard to convince people that your father would never have taken it, but that somehow it got lost. It worried her that so many wouldn't accept that idea."

"Did the bank, I mean the men from Bangor, ask her questions?"

"Of course. They questioned everybody, even me, who hadn't been near the bank for weeks. Alice was always nervous and timid, the last person to stand up under questioning, but

Vince said she answered everything and just kept putting in: 'But George never would take the bank money. It got into the water and went out with the tide. It must have.'"

"When did she get sick?"

"She was sick then, though none of us knew it. I think she even knew she wouldn't get well. She had gone to Portland a few weeks before that, and later we found that she had gone to a doctor there. But it was months before she died. She was still in the bank for a while, then too sick to work, and finally too sick to do anything. That was when Liza took care of her. Poor Alice! She felt the trouble we were in so much."

"Was Annie the same then as she is now?"

"Just the same, I think, though I haven't seen her since we came back."

"I have," said Georgia. "I went to see her. I think she's batty."

"She always was—queer, I mean. And I don't think she, or anybody, knows anything that you can find out. Maybe the money did wash away with the tide, as Alice always said. Or if it didn't I don't think you can ever find out what did happen. Plenty of people have tried." She leaned over to adjust the flame of the reading lamp, and took up her book.

"There's just one thing to do, daughter, for either you or me. Make people accept us for what we are ourselves, if there are any that don't do that now. And don't dig into the past. There's nothing but disappointment there. I tried it too."

Georgia was quiet, but she was far from accepting her mother's advice.

"I can't! I can't!" she said to herself. "I've got to find out!"

CHAPTER 15

THE BARN

Herb presented himself for work as he had agreed.

"He must have got his strength back, or got caught up on his reading, or both," Georgia said to her mother as they saw his car turning in from the road. "And we're all ready for him, aren't we?"

"All ready," said her mother. "I hope we aren't going to miss the heat here when we've moved the big stove out."

"It's summer," said Georgia. "And besides, there's the stove we took out when we opened the fireplace. We could put that in here."

"Yes, if that wouldn't 'run afoul,' as Uncle Joshua used to say, of my daughter's prejudice against stoves."

"Oh, stoves have their uses," said Georgia airily.

By this time they could hear Herb bumping his way along with his heavy tool case, and Georgia ran to open the door for him.

"Now what's this crazy notion you've got this time?" he began, with no preliminary greetings other than a stiff nod in answer to their good mornings.

Georgia was all ready to take up battle with him, but her

mother shook her head from behind Herb's shoulder as he set the tool case down.

"Don't you remember, Herb," she said, "that the little room back of this used to be 'the sink room' or 'the butt'ry' or something like that? There wasn't any sink in here when I first began to come to visit."

"Well, where you going to put the sink if you take it out of here?" He was already at the door into the back room, refusing, it seemed, to be drawn into any sentimental remembrances. "Lucky they ain't any fancy plumbing to move. Don't know as I'd let you do that."

Yes, he admitted, the sink could go under the west window in the butt'ry, and there would be plenty of room for shelves 'n' things on the two inside walls. But the stove! The chimney was between that room and the kitchen, and he talked learnedly about flues, about good drafts and poor drafts, about ovens that baked and ovens that wouldn't heat up, nohow.

"Oh, you can do it, Herb," said Mrs. Lane. "Of course I don't know about these things, but you do." And Herb agreed that he did, knew all about them, in fact.

"I can do it, if it can be done," he said, and they left him to begin work. They stacked the dishes which they could not wash now until the sink was newly placed. They would leave Herb a clear field.

He opened the seldom used doors from the butt'ry to the outdoors, one on the front and one on the back of the house, flooding the prospective kitchen with light and fresh morning air.

"Look, Mums," said Georgia. "It's going to be perfect."

"Fine," said her mother. "Now what are you going to do this morning, so you will keep out of Herb's way?"

"I thought I'd take care of the clothes I dumped on the porch chamber bed, Lucy Lorenzo's bonnet and the other things. When Lorrie gets here, we'll dress up someday and let you see what the well-dressed ancestor wears. And then, after that —I mean after I put them away somewhere this morning—Vee said maybe he'd come down and we'd row across the bay. I want to see what's over there."

"Just about the same as on this side, probably," said Mrs. Lane. "But you'll like rowing over. There used to be a nice little rowboat here. It might be stored in the barn still. We'll have a look."

"I'll look now," and Georgia dashed off, quite regardless of morning dew and wet grass. She had not really investigated the barn at all yet. There might be other things there she would like to see, as well as a possible boat.

The barn, unlike most barns in this colder end of Maine, was not attached to the house, but stood somewhat apart, stark and gray, and leaning a little with age. The big doors were fastened together only by a short stick thrust through a rusty staple, and they rolled back easily enough when Georgia pulled out the stick and put her strength into a push. Indeed she was surprised at the smooth action of such big doors.

Inside the barn, it was shadowy and smelled of hay, but as the doors, one after the other, rolled back, a shaft of morning sunlight lighted up the interior. Georgia looked about curiously.

"I guess I don't know anything about barns," she said.

"I guess you don't," said Vee's voice behind her, making her jump with surprise.

"Susie says you're looking for a boat," he went on. "It isn't here, though. It's moored up back of my house. Uncle Josh gave it to me years ago. He said he'd never use it any more, his joints had got too stiff. I've had a lot of fun in it, and now if you're a good girl, maybe you can have fun too."

Georgia hardly listened. It was all right about the boat, she thought vaguely, but what she wanted now to know was about barns, and the cobwebby treasures that lurked in the corners of this one. "Tell me about these things," she said.

"Well," said Vee, "here where the big doors open is where the hayracks get driven in, so the hay can be pitched up to the mows, on either side. You know about haymows, don't you?"

"No," said Georgia, "but I can see where they are. What's all the rest of the space for?"

"Over there's the tie-up," and he waved toward the fenced-off section on their left. "Uncle Josh used to have eight or ten cows in there."

"Tie-up," said Georgia. "It was the cows they tied up?" And she walked down in front of the long space devoted to them, trying to imagine friendly brown-eyed cows looking out at her over the barrier. "What about these little rooms at the end?" she asked.

"Stalls, not rooms," said Vee with an amused smile. "Stalls, for horses." Georgia accepted this information, and turned sharply toward the other side. "What's over here?"

That side had a partition all the way up to the haymow, with only a small door near the front.

"The carriage house," said Vee, and he went over to open the small door.

"Oh, I hope—" said Georgia as she followed him to the doorway. Then she squealed with delight. "That's a sleigh," she said. "I've seen plenty of those in pictures. Santa Claus rides in one."

"Sure does," said Vee. "Other folks do, too, even now. If they haven't got cars, or their roads don't get plowed out. But mostly," he added with pride, "even on the Hackmatack road, you can drive your car all winter."

"If you've got the car," said Georgia. She walked on into the dimly lighted carriage house. "Is that a buggy?" she asked. "I've been hearing about buggy rides all my life."

"No, that's a surrey. They used to call it a carryall, and they'd pack the whole family into it, for church or to go visiting."

"How do you know so much about it? You couldn't ever have ridden in one of these," declared Georgia.

"I could have, but I probably never did. There are plenty of people in Lane's Cove who have, though. And besides, I'm a transportation man. They didn't always have railroads, and I've read about how they got around before that. You ought to see the old stagecoach that stands in the middle of the station at Concord, New Hampshire. I went up there from Boston just to see it. The Concord Coach, they called it, because they made them there."

"When were you in Boston?" Georgia asked.

"Dad took me, one Christmas vacation." He laughed. "He let me hang around the big stations all I wanted to, and I went on trips, like the one to Concord. I had a wonderful time."

"Is that all you saw of Boston?"

"It's what I wanted to see," declared Vee.

Georgia turned back to the carryall. "This has a top like an old four-poster bed," she said. "With that funny little fringe for curtains. I've seen pictures of old beds. But isn't there a buggy?" She sounded disappointed.

"Sure. Buggies didn't carry all, they carried two. Fellows

took their girls to ride. Here's one," and he led her beyond the surrey.

"I like that," said Georgia, noticing the slender spokes in the wheels, the small body balanced on springs. "It's light, and graceful." Then looking at more shadowy vehicles in the corners, once more she asked, "Didn't they ever throw anything away?"

"Not much, I'd say. Aunt Susan liked to keep things. The old hayracks and wagons—"

They walked toward the big side door where the carriages went in and out.

"I was going to say," Vee began again, "that the old farm wagons fell to pieces after Uncle Josh stopped farming and they'd stood out in the weather. But Aunt Susan wouldn't get rid of the carriages in here to make room for the others, so they just rotted away."

"We ought to have a museum," said Georgia.

"We have," answered Vee, "sort of one. Lane House."

"It's funny to be born in a museum," said Georgia.

"It wasn't a museum then," Vee answered comfortably, "though it was something like this. The Lanes never threw things away either."

But Georgia's mood of happy investigation was broken. "Come on," she said. "Let's row across the bay."

By the time Herb had finished his day's work both sink and stove had been placed, and tomorrow he would begin building the new shelves and cupboards. The parlor stove displaced from the living room and taken the place of the big cookstove in what would now be the dining room—and study, Georgia insisted. A fire was laid in it ready to light if a "no'theaster" made the weather cold and raw, and a fire was already burning in the new kitchen, to heat the dishwater and cook the supper. Pom accepted the change at once and had followed the fire, lying now at full length in front of the oven door.

"We do get things done," said Mrs. Lane. "I wouldn't have believed these few changes would make so much difference."

Georgia made no reply. She was thinking: "We do get things done, all but the biggest thing of all, the one that would give me a chance to be happy in Lane's Cove. Me, and Mums, too."

"Forget it, Georgia," said her mother quietly. Mums knew what she was thinking, because Mums was thinking the same thing herself.

Georgia roused and rather forcibly pulled her thoughts back to the new kitchen, to Lorraine's coming, and the strangeness of expecting Mrs. Allerton. If she could only be as happy all of the time as she was some of it. If she could only find the answer to that one question. Then she could accept Lane's Cove and be happy in it.

Another day of Herb's work and the room was ready for paint and the arranging of dishes and supplies. Georgia was cheerful again, and found a good deal of pleasure in relieving the old shelves and cupboards in the large room of kitchen things, leaving space to spread out the old china to better advantage.

"The open shelves can be for books and magazines and things like that now," Georgia said, "and a little radio, when we can afford the battery kind. Vee says we should have brought the electric one, and Johnnie Phillips might have made it over. Johnnie plays with radio the way Vee does with railroads." She set the old pink willow sugar bowl on one of the shelves and stood back to get the effect.

"The boys around here have hobbies, but the girls don't seem to play with anything at all," she continued, moving the sugar bowl to another place, where it would show off better.

"You don't know yet what they play with," said her mother. "There's the Summer Club. That will give them something to do."

"I wonder if their show will be just another Talent Night over again."

"Propose something else," said Mrs. Lane.

"Me?" said Georgia. "Who's going to listen to me? I can hear Mona's crowd now squashing anything I propose."

"What's wrong between you and Mona? Her people used to be friends of ours."

"Have you seen them since we came back?"

"Yes, her father and mother talked to me after church one Sunday. They said they were coming down."

"They did?" A frown puckered Georgia's brows.

"Why not?" Mrs. Lane's face clouded. "Were you thinking—"

"I was thinking of what Mona said. That her father crossed my father's name off his list of friends." Georgia had not meant to tell, but it was out now.

"Oh, no," said Mrs. Lane.

That was all, just "Oh, no." But Georgia could feel the doubt creeping into her mother's voice. If Mona had lied about it—probably she had lied about it, and that was why she was so fierce in her dislike of Georgia. She had to remember the lie.

And if she had lied about it, probably the reason was what Edwina had said. It was all because Vee hadn't gone back home with Mona that first Sunday afternoon when they had all gone to ride. And because Mona had had to sit on the back seat with Curt that day, instead of with Vee in front. Fathers hadn't anything to do with it at all. Was there really anybody that thought George Lane had taken the money, except Herb? And what did he know about it? Besides, what did Herb count for, here in Lane's Cove? He would always have a grievance, that or another.

Next morning, while she was painting shelves, screwing in cup hooks and making plans as to the most convenient places for things, she made up her mind that she would take her mother's advice. "Forget it, Georgia," Mums had said. And once before, "We must make people accept us for what we are ourselves." Mums was probably right.

By Monday noon the new kitchen was done. Georgia had selected the colors for the paint, soft green for the woodwork and a cheerful yellow for the walls. She had hated waiting for the paint to get fully dry and had tested with an experimental finger any number of times. But now everything was finished, every saucepan and kettle hung in its appointed place, bowls placed in orderly rows on the shelves, sugar and flour in Aunt Susan's old wooden firkins, even the little spice jars on the narrow shelf Herb had protestingly built at Georgia's order.

"Nonsense," he said, even as he sawed and planed the three inch board to make the shelf, "might as well have it twice as wide. Wider shelf, double row of things."

"I don't want a double row," Georgia had answered. "I don't like poking around to find out what I want."

"Suit yourself," said Herb sourly. "No economy in wasting space, though."

Georgia was glad that Herb's job was done and she did not have to listen to his complaining, but she wished he could see how things looked. He would have to think the room was a success.

"Mums," she called, "come and look at it once more. I keep coming back. What would I do if I planned rooms for somebody else and then couldn't see them any more after they were done?"

"What would you do if you painted a picture and sold it?"

"Awful!" Georgia gave an exaggerated shudder, and went over to straighten one of the short ruffled curtains over the window behind the sink. Then they both went upstairs.

Lorraine was to have the room across the front stairway from Georgia's. That looked neat and tidy, too, though Georgia sighed for new wallpaper, as she did for all the upstairs rooms.

"Something that isn't *practical*," she said to her mother, who laughed.

"Next year, maybe," Mrs. Lane said. "I think we've spent our quota on the house for this year."

Next year! It looked far away to Georgia. Between her and next summer lay a long cold winter, a whole school year, with Mona to endure, and without Vee to make things easier for her. She would miss Vee. She wondered how she would get to school next year, and whether Mona's enmity would die down when Vee was gone. She wished Mona's father and mother would make that promised call.

Then she went to her room, making haste with getting cleaned up, tossing off the old paint-stained gingham she had worn during what she had called "the kitchen campaign," splashing water into the rose-patterned bowl, brushing vigorously at her tousled hair.

One of the new summer dresses her mother had bought for her before they left Boston lay on the bed. A plain little dress, but crisp and new. There had not been much weather for real summer dresses so far.

She was dressed and ready some time before Vee would probably come, and wandered in and out of the downstairs rooms while she waited. She hoped Mrs. Allerton wouldn't be cold in there by those north windows. There was bright sun in the living room, and she opened all the doors so the heat would get into the bedroom.

Mrs. Lane was doing some last thing in the kitchen, then came in to say: "I knew that dull yellow would be a good color for you, the minute I saw the dress. Stop trotting around and let me look. I'm glad you are taking the brown sweater along. If it gets chilly, that will keep you warm and match your eyes, too. I think I hear Vee coming down the road." She picked up her coat and they both went out through what was now the dining-room door.

The errands took quite a time. It was always slow work when they shopped at Tillie's, because Tillie was much happier to talk, especially to Mums, Georgia thought, than to be measuring out molasses or hunting on the upper shelves for something "I know I've got, but can't seem to remember just where'bouts it is."

Sometimes Georgia went in and stood around during the long conversations, but today she sat outside in the car. When Mrs. Lane appeared at the door, Vee went in to bring out the packages, and while he was busy with them at the back of the car, Georgia heard the long wail of the train whistle.

"Oh, Vee," she called, "we ought to hurry. I hear the train."

"Plenty of time," he answered. "That's way over beyond Woodbridge. Six minutes yet, even if she's on time. Bet you we'll sit around and wait three times that before she gets here." He came around the car calmly, got in and made a leisurely start up Main Street toward the station.

They did wait, and though Mrs. Lane and Vee could converse easily and contentedly, Georgia could put her mind on nothing but the long-drawn whistle, a little louder each time, and at last just around the bend of the track beyond the station. The stationmaster, whom Georgia remembered from that day when they had first come, rattled a baggage truck up the platform, and the man arrived with the mail just in time.

"Thar she blows!" said Vee, and the slowing *chug chug* of the train brought it to its grinding stop. Georgia ran along the platform to the spot where the conductor had stepped down and was reaching up to give a hand to the first passenger to alight. It was Mrs. Allerton, and behind her Lorraine, tugging two heavy suitcases.

"She would take them both," Mrs. Allerton protested, as the conductor took first one and then the other and set them firmly on the platform.

"Quite right, ma'am, quite right," said the conductor. "Glad to see some manners in the young. Not too much these days."

A few other passengers straggled behind. Freight was bumping on the platform up ahead, mailbags thudding, and the old engine breathing hard in convulsive gasps. Georgia was half-conscious of these sounds, but only half. Her mother had reached the spot and was greeting Mrs. Allerton. Vee was there, too, grasping both suitcases, and she herself was saying, "Lorrie, this is Vee," and then looking from one to the other as they both grinned cheerfully and said, "Hi," in the same breath.

She realized suddenly that they were the same kind of people, Lorrie and Vee. They would like each other, of course. They might like each other very much. And how would she feel about that?

CHAPTER 16

CLUB MEETING

By Wednesday, the day of the club meeting, the two girls seemed to have bridged most of the gaps caused by their weeks of separation. That first evening, while Mrs. Allerton and Mrs. Lane had sat before the fire in the living room, Georgia and Lorraine had laughed and chattered on the old sofa, with excursions here and there, to see Pom, the sunset, the birches and the view through to the bay, the wide fields beyond the garden on the south side of the house. They even went out for a quick glimpse at the dim recesses of the barn and carriage house, the buggy and the carryall.

"You do like it here," said Lorraine. "I knew you would. Remember what I told you?"

"Yes," said Georgia. "And I think you said it again in every letter you wrote. I do like some things, a lot better than I thought I should. But—" she stopped there and reached for Pom, who had followed them in and was rubbing around her ankles.

"Come, Pom," she said. "Let Lorrie see how silky your coat is." And she lifted Pom up to Lorraine's lap to be smoothed and cuddled.

When bedtime came they were not talked out, and Georgia was quite ready to accept Lorraine's invitation to share the big bed in Lorraine's room.

"But don't talk all night," said Mrs. Lane.

"We won't. It will be like that night at your house," Lorraine said, turning to Mrs. Allerton. "That seems a long time ago, doesn't it?"

"It does indeed," said Mrs. Allerton. "Before the emancipation, in a way of speaking."

Georgia was not quite sure what ought to be said to that, but Lorraine answered promptly by asking another question.

"How did you happen to ask us that night?" she said.

"I'd been getting ready to do something like that for a long time, I can see now," said Mrs. Allerton. "Nursing a grievance, all by yourself, isn't really a satisfying way to live." She looked around at all of them.

"I needed people, and finally I came to see it. So in a reckless moment I reached out to get some." She laughed as she added: "It was a venture, and probably I thought I wasn't taking much of a chance. In a few hours you'd be going away."

"But not me," said Lorraine. "You forgot that I'd be there and come pushing in to upset your life."

"It needed upsetting. I was glad when you came."

"And now you're here—" Lorraine began.

"And have some new friends," Mrs. Allerton finished.

Later, when Lorraine had been instructed how to put out the light of the kerosene lamp, and they were both tucked in snugly under the blankets and the log-cabin quilt, Georgia brought up the subject again.

"We didn't really find out what made her do it. Never go out, I mean, and hide herself away like a hermit."

Lorraine had to stifle quick laughter and lower her voice as she answered. "That's the joke on us," she said. "We were dopey, all right. The whole street was dopey. She didn't hide herself, the way we thought, except just from us. We weren't her kind, and she hated us because we weren't. So she stuck her head up high and acted just as if she didn't live there any more."

"Why didn't she move somewhere else? She could have, couldn't she?"

"Well," said Lorraine again, this time reflectively, "maybe she was a little queer, or stubborn anyway. It was her home, she liked it, and she was used to it. So she stayed."

There was a minute of silence, then Georgia said, "Locking the door on Kendall Street didn't hurt anybody but her, did it?"

"I guess she knows that now," said Lorraine.

Mrs. Allerton fitted easily into the ways of the household, taking little walks through the birches to the shore, sitting for hours in the sun with a book in her lap, even offering after a day or two to help Mrs. Lane in the garden.

"One of those quiet people," said Georgia.

"She's had plenty of practice," Lorraine answered. "Unless she talked to herself."

Wednesday afternoon, the two girls were ready to walk to the village for the first meeting of the Summer Club. The early dinner, promptly at noon, was over and the dishes washed. Georgia had put on the dull yellow dress and Lorraine a rose-colored one that Georgia had not seen before.

"It looks just right with your black hair," said Georgia. "I've always wished my hair was black."

"I'd change for your dusty brown," said Lorraine. "Or better yet, for that pale corn color."

"Like Mona's," said Georgia. "Come on, let's start now or we'll overtake her on the road. And I certainly don't intend to let that happen."

"Don't you like Mona?" asked Lorraine as they walked along. "And why didn't I ever hear about her before?"

"I didn't tell you about her because I don't like her and I don't like to think about her. If I could lock her out the way Mrs. Allerton did Kendall Street—"

"Oh, no, you don't want to be queer, do you? What's the matter with her, anyway?"

This was the time, Georgia decided, to tell Lorraine whatever she needed to know, to forestall the gossip she was sure to hear, the guarded remarks that Mona's crowd would be certain to make. Besides, it would help, just to talk it over with Lorrie. Perhaps, together, they could think of some way. Georgia was beginning to be sure that she could not, alone.

The walk seemed shorter to her today, and they were in the village by the time the story was finished. Lorraine had made little comment on the connection of Georgia's father with the bank loss. That wasn't like Lorraine, so Georgia knew that she was disturbed, perhaps a little embarrassed, by what she heard.

"He didn't take it, Lorrie," Georgia said. "You must believe that."

"Of course. I don't wonder you dreaded coming back."

The story of Mona and her friends had been easier to tell. School hadn't been bad at all, except for her, "but from that very first day when we went to ride and she got so raging mad, she's never lost a chance. And that gang of hers, just the same. They hang around, waiting to laugh every time she sticks a pin into me. I get the jitters, Lorrie."

Lorraine's reaction to Mona's attitude was fully satisfying.

That was quite within her experience, and Lorrie never lacked words to express what she felt about things she knew. She was still on the subject when they reached Edwina's house, an old white one on Hill Street, not far from Cove Bridge.

Other girls began to arrive, one at a time or in groups. Georgia and Lorraine sat back in the room to which Edwina had taken them, and watched the room fill up.

"There won't be chairs enough, girls," said Edwina. "If you don't mind, we could sit outdoors." And they all trooped out, to distribute themselves on the grass.

"Twenty-seven," Edwina counted, including Mona and four of her friends who had just appeared.

"Had to walk all the way," said Mona as she dropped into a spot in the shade of the house. "I call it hot."

"This is a *meeting,*" Edwina began. "Who's going to be the head of it?"

"You are," said somebody near the back of the group. "It's your house."

"Nothing to that," said Edwina firmly. "We have to elect someone."

"Okay, we'll elect you." And, driven to the exertion, they did make a motion, second it, and vote, all in record time.

"Unanimous," said Mag. "Now you sit up there in the big lawn chair, Eddie, and start the ball rolling. Secretary, treasurer, and all that. Then we can get down to business and decide what we're going to do this year."

Nobody wanted to be secretary, but after two or three had been nominated and had declined, Mag agreed to do it. "We have to have one, I suppose," she said, "but we don't run to minutes of meetings and that kind of thing. It won't ruin me, I guess."

The treasurer came next, and someone nominated Georgia.

"Treasurer?" said Mona softly to her next neighbor on the grass, but not softly enough for the neighbor's ears alone. "That isn't such a good idea." And they both laughed under their breaths.

Lorraine, who had already identified Mona by the "pale, corn-colored hair," was near enough to hear, and so was Georgia. How many others heard Georgia could only guess.

After she, with slightly heightened color, had declined the nomination and two or three others had done the same, the proposal that Mag should be both treasurer and secretary was made, and Mag finally agreed.

"There won't be much money to handle except for the show," she said resignedly, "and for that I'll get somebody that's really smart to help me. One of the boys, maybe."

"Now that's out of the way," said Edwina, "the only thing we have to decide right away is what we're going to do this year. Have fun, of course. That's one thing the club is for. But there's the show, what the money's to be for this time, and what kind of show we can have. I'd like it to be a knockout this year, and I hope everybody is chock-full of ideas." She paused, waiting apparently for ideas to sprout at once from the minds of the girls sitting cross-legged on the grass before her.

There was a dead silence. Finally someone said: "Trouble is, everybody's done the same things so many times."

"I suppose," a second girl said doubtfully, "we might have a play."

"Awful lot of work," another girl added. "And nobody to coach us that's any good. If Chet Lindsay wasn't going to that summer school—"

"But he is," Mag said. "I think a play's out."

Georgia and Lorraine sat listening but taking no part in the discussion. Now, however, Edwina turned to them to say: "What about you, George? And, girls, remember that Lorraine Fitzgerald, George's friend, is from Boston, too. What do Boston girls do when they want to make some money? You must remember something?"

"The same kinds of things they do everywhere," said Lorraine. "Sing, recite, have plays, operettas, dance revues. I'd say there isn't anything that's very new."

"Something might be new to Lane's Cove, though," Edwina commented.

"Once our vacation club had a pet show," Georgia said. "But that was in the daytime and nobody much came except ourselves. It was fun, but it wasn't a money-maker."

"There was the fashion show," Lorraine reminded her. "That did make money, but we didn't do it alone. You can't have a fashion show without the new fashions," she explained, "and one of the big stores put it on for us. We wore the things, and sold the tickets, and our share of the money went to Junior Red Cross. That was fun, too."

"I'd love to see the new styles, outside of some mail-order catalogue or the movies," said one of the Harwood girls, who, Georgia remembered, seemed to have more clothes than most of the girls. "But of course that's out."

There was another of those silences. Then Georgia said, hesitating a little: "I've got an idea. But I don't know whether it's any good or not. Maybe you'll think it's silly." By that time she was wishing she had said nothing at all, but every eye was on her, and she had to go on. "It's about clothes," she said, "but not about new ones. We've been finding old things, Lucy Lorenzo's bonnet and things like that—"

"Lucy Lorenzo's bonnet!" Mona kept her derisive laughter low, but Georgia heard it, and Mona's friends heard it, it seemed, and echoed it promptly. And somebody else said, "Lucy Lorenzo's bonnet?" in honest bewilderment. "Who was Lucy Lorenzo?"

"It's just an old bonnet, from long ago," Georgia explained, "but I thought it was pretty when I tried it on. There are old silk dresses, and hoop skirts, and oh, everything. They were in the closets and in the attic. I wouldn't let my mother throw them away, and she said that probably every attic in town had things like them, or better. Why couldn't we wear the things and have an *Ancestors' Fashion Show?*"

"We've got a whole set of baby clothes, dresses yards long, with bushels of lace and tucks," said someone.

"Well, we could borrow a baby," said Mag.

"And I know where there's a trunkful of wonderful Civil War clothes," someone else said, "soldiers' uniforms, dresses with wide sleeves and lace undersleeves, and all sorts of things. The girls' dresses look just like the ones in the movie of *Little Women.*"

"My great-great-grandfather's stovepipe hat is in our attic," a third girl put in. "We used it once in a play. And those funny tight pants they wore, that had straps going under the sole of the shoe."

"Our house doesn't go back that far," Mag laughed, "but I've got a hobble skirt that Gran wore. I put it on, and actually, you can't *step.*"

"The treasure in our attic," said another, "is my grandmother's first evening dress. That was sometime in the last of the nineties, and she wore it to a ball in New York. Her father sailed out of New York and she lived there for a while. It has puffed sleeves that won't let you go through a door without turning sideways."

"Honest? And they think the things we wear are queer."

Everybody was talking at once, and Edwina had to rap sharply for order. She pulled off a shoe and used its heel to pound on the arm of the big lawn chair. The voices died away.

"Maybe we've got something there," she said. "Let's all poke around our attics and report when we meet next week. I know there's a very fancy pair of slippers that somebody in my family wore, all seed pearls and things. But I couldn't get my feet into them. Perhaps Mona might."

"I'm not sure I'd want to," said Mona. "It sounds like a crazy idea to me. Who'd want to pay money to see those old things? That isn't my idea of a show."

"Not if you could sing *Listen to the Mockingbird* in the costume of the period?" That was Mary Harwood. "Besides, it would give those of us who can't do anything a chance to stand up and be looked at for once in our lives. I'm all for it."

"No harm to hunt and see what we've got," said Mag. "And, Eddie, I move that you appoint a committee, and that next week we decide. We can meet at my house next time."

The committee was appointed, with Georgia as chairman, and then business was laid aside. "Next week," said Edwina, "I hope there'll be time enough left to play something, but today we'll have to go from here straight to the ice cream and chocolate cake."

"That's all right with me, Eddie," said Mag. "Your mother makes wonderful chocolate cake. I hope there's plenty."

When they all left, at once, to go home, Georgia held back until she was sure Mona had plenty of "head start."

"Too bad she has to live on our road," she said to Lorraine as they set out, and she told about the day Mona had walked along ahead of her and Curt had dismissed Mona with his gruff, "Good-by."

"I thought she was simply poisonous," said Lorraine. "I could have wrung her neck when she said that."

"I'd have liked to stick a knife into her and twist it," Georgia replied fiercely. "And there isn't one thing I can do." She stamped across Cove Bridge as if Mona's head were under each heel she brought down.

"I want to see Lucy Lorenzo's bonnet," said Lorraine. "Who was she anyhow? If she lived in Kendall Street, we'd say she was Italian."

"She wasn't. It was her husband who was Lorenzo, and he wasn't Italian either. Just one of those funny names people down here used to like to tack on their children." Georgia forgot Mona, as she thought of the old names.

"We've got the old Burnham family Bible," she went on, "where they list everybody's name as soon as he's born and has one. There are some of the weirdest names. Lucretia, Aurianna, Vashti, Aubine. They were all my great-grandmother's sisters. The boys' names aren't so funny. They are mostly John, James, Henry. Things like that, except Lorenzo, and Azro. They were twins, long, long ago, and I guess their mother let herself go when she named them."

"What do you suppose they'll do about the show?" asked Lorraine. "That was a super idea you had, and I hope they'll use it."

"One minute I hope so, too, and then the next minute I wish I had kept my tongue very, very still. Mona'll be after my hide, and if she could queer the whole thing she would, because I thought of it."

The road to the Corners was pleasant in the late afternoon and they walked along briskly. Georgia showed Lorraine the swampy place in the heath where the pitcher plants and the lady slippers grew, adding: "I'd go in and get some, if I didn't have on good shoes. We'll come up someday, dressed for it in dungarees and rubber boots."

They had almost reached the Corners when Georgia said: "I thought Vee might come up and bring us home. He knew the club was today."

"I don't mind walking," said Lorraine. "Do you see a lot of Vee?"

"Not so much now school is over," said Georgia. And even as she spoke, a car came up behind them, slowed down, and Vee's voice called, "Ride, wenches?" as he pulled it to a stop.

That was fine, except that Mona was settled in the front seat. "I can't keep away from the poison bug," Georgia muttered, but there was nothing to do but open the back door and wave Lorraine in ahead of her. But, glory be, Mona wouldn't be going far.

In another two minutes they were at the Fairchild lane and after that Mona was soon disposed of.

"Come in front?" said Vee. "Room for three, all right."

"It isn't far enough to pay to move," Georgia answered.

"Okay, you're the boss," said Vee. "Been hearing about the next Summer Club show. You're going to boss that too, I hear."

"I wouldn't pay too much attention to what you hear from that source." Georgia tried to make her voice cold and smooth, but it wasn't easy. The contempt in Mona's *"Treasurer? That isn't such a good idea,"* still rankled. How did she dare say things like that?

Vee laughed. "And I wouldn't pay too much attention to

her if I were you either. Don't you know green eyes when you see them? I hope you boss the show and that it's the best one the Club ever had. There, could anybody say more than that?"

He turned farther from the wheel to catch Lorraine's eye. "What do you think of Hackmatack, so far?" He was clearly trying to be agreeable, but his attention had to go back to his driving before Lorraine could answer.

She leaned forward and said emphatically: "I like it fine, all except that dainty package you've just delivered up the road. Where I live, I think they'd drop her in the Charles. Or maybe that's wishful thinking." And she went on to echo Georgia's own thought, "How does she dare to say things like that?"

"Like what?"

"Never mind, Lorrie." Georgia could not bear to hear it again. "And, Vee, next time you have her in the car, don't stop to pick me up. I don't want to boss the show, unless—" and to her own astonishment as well as that of the others, she burst into violent weeping.

CHAPTER 17

ANCESTORS' FASHIONS

"It can't be as bad as all that," said Vee, when he had stopped the car, and Georgia had mumbled from the depths of her handkerchief, "Sorry. I certainly didn't mean to slop over like that."

"Can't you see?" said Lorraine, looking fiercely at Vee. "It's bad enough to ruin everything. When she could be so happy here, too. But she never will be, unless—"

"Unless what?" Vee interrupted coolly. Then he leaned over the back of the front seat toward Georgia. "You think I'm all sorts of things because I won't help you keep struggling to find out what happened in the bank. And you think Dad's mean, and a pretty bad best friend, because he didn't ever prove your father was all right, and because he won't help you now. What you don't see is that Dad wouldn't ever have stopped trying without a good reason."

His glance swept over to include Lorraine too. "And what my Dad can't find out is, just as he said; nothing for kids to mix into."

"He didn't ever find that diary of Alice's, did he?" Georgia's voice was still tremulous.

"Annie has the diary. You saw it," said Vee to her shortly.

"No, I mean the other one—"

"That Liza says Alice had? Nobody's ever seen that. Alice probably burned it up."

"That's what Liza said," Georgia admitted. "I'm all right now, Vee. You can go on."

Vee, however, backed the car into the alders at the side of the road, turned after some maneuvering, and started back up the road to the Corners.

"No hurry, is there?" he said. "Take a little ride, round the square, maybe." And Georgia remembered the other time that he had taken her round the square when Mona had been hateful.

"Funny," he said now. "Mona used to be a decent kid. I thought so anyway." Then he stopped the car once more. "Get in front, you two," he said gruffly. "I'm getting a permanent twist in my neck. Plenty of room here for three."

For a few minutes they rode in silence, then Lorraine announced decisively, "We've got to *do something.*"

"Yeah," said Vee. "The way they say around here, 'They ought to be a law.' But I don't know any way to stop gossip, and if little George," he said with heavy emphasis, slowing down the car so he could give his whole attention to Lorraine, "if little George lets one half-pint kid ruin her life, the way you say, you and I can't do anything about it. It's up to her."

"What would you do?" snapped Lorraine. "I'd just like to know that."

"Me? I'd boss the Summer Club show, just as if the kid was no more than one of the midges that swarm down on the shore when the sun's hot. And I'd make that show the best darn show the Club ever had. And I'd stand up tall and look straight over the top of half-pint's head. That'd hurt her more than any-thing, if hurting her's what you want to do."

"I'd hate to have my fingers in that handsome hair of hers," said Georgia. "She wouldn't have so much when I got through."

"Ho! Sort of a wildcat, ain't—I mean aren't—you? Well, what say? Do the show, no matter what?"

"I suppose so," said Georgia, a little sulkily. "But I hope she keeps out of my way."

"She'd better, from what you say. Now, instead of going round the square, suppose we keep on through Woodbridge, down to Fountain Rocks. You ought to see that. It's one of our sightliest places."

Not far beyond Woodbridge, they turned onto the Fountain Rocks Road, running for miles close to the shore. Massive rocks, shingle beaches on its shore side, on the other towering pines with only a bare footing in thin soil over the ledges, many of them twisted into strange shapes by the constant battering of winter sea winds.

There were no houses, only here and there in some sheltered cove a lone fisherman's shack, with lobster traps piled high on the broken clam shells around it, and the sharp reek of fish in the air. Then the road came to an end at the very tip of the long point. Nothing now but rocks and open sea, and a far-off dim horizon. Rocks in huge misshapen piles, a mile or two across, behind which the sea rolled and broke high in frothy spray.

There seemed nothing to say in a place like that, so they sat in silence, watching the great waves gather, strike with a roar, spring high in foam, and settle back in sullen power. But finally Vee stirred.

"It isn't always like that," he said. "Makes a difference how the wind's been for a couple of days. Sometime we'll get a gang together, come over and stay long enough to build a fire on the rocks and cook a chowder." He pushed the starter, and as the engine caught, put the car slowly into motion, with a last look at a great fountain of water thrown up by a huge wave.

"Now we'd better be on our way," he went on. "Not too much time to get to the pasture bars ahead of the cows. They have the darnedest sense of time, always on the dot."

Fountain Rocks was good medicine, Georgia knew, for the misery that had threatened to engulf her, and she came back with courage renewed and with a determination to make her fight regardless of anything Mona might do or say.

Next morning, Georgia called Lorraine to attack with her the problem of "ancestors' fashions" as exemplified in the heap on the bed in the porch chamber.

"It's a bigger job than any of us thought." Georgia was sitting in the midst of garments of all sorts, and completely at sea as to the period in which each of them had been worn.

"Well," said Lorraine, "start with the bonnet. When did Lucy Lorenzo live?"

"The Burnham Bible will tell us that." Georgia swept the lapful of clothes aside. "But we need to know other things besides that or we'll have nothing but a hodgepodge." They both clattered downstairs to consult the old Bible.

"There must be somebody that knows about old fashions," said Lorraine, as they scanned the pages in the middle of the big Bible, on which the long record of births, marriages and deaths had been written in.

"How about that State Library?" suggested Mrs. Lane, passing through the room on the way to the stairs. "There must be books there about what people wore."

"I'll write a letter to them before the mailman comes this afternoon," said Georgia. "Maybe I'll get an answer before the next club meeting. Come on, Lorrie, and bring a pencil. We'll make a list of what we've got here. Lucy Lorenzo was married in 1849."

"I wonder what the other girls will find," said Georgia, when they had finished the list and had hung the old garments carefully on hangers in the porch chamber. "Most of these things aren't so very good. They had to wear them too much, and too long. They couldn't find new ones to buy as easily as we do."

"Even if they had the money to buy them with," said Lorraine. "That's why the silks are cracked on the seams, and why some of the things are that funny homespun, with queer colors."

"They probably had to dye them themselves. I hope the other girls find plenty. We'll need a lot to choose from."

"Don't forget the baby clothes," reminded Lorraine, "and the Civil War uniforms." They both laughed.

"There's another thing," said Georgia. "How are we going to let the audience know about who wore the clothes, and when? We can't hang placards on the models."

"We could have it all written down about each one, and then somebody could announce them as they come out," suggested Lorraine.

"It sounds like a lot of work," said Georgia doubtfully.

"Well, you've got a committee. Divide it up and make everybody work. And don't forget to write to that State Library."

"Oh, no, we'll do it now," said Georgia, and they clattered down the stairs again.

"Hi, Aunt Martha," said Georgia, finding Mrs. Allen sitting with Mrs. Lane and Mrs. Allerton in the dining room, when

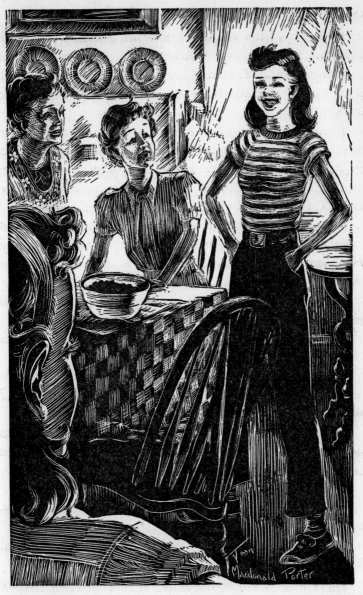

*"Mrs. Allerton wouldn't unlock the door," Lorraine said
suddenly.*

she rushed in to get paper and pen from a shelf. All three were sociably picking over wild strawberries.

"Didn't expect to see me here in the middle of a morning, did you?" said Mrs. Allen. "I wouldn't be, if I hadn't had to ask your mother something. And now I'm here, I just sit. It's a nice place to do that."

The two girls laughed when they were safely out of sight and hearing. "Did you see Mrs. Allerton? Would you believe it?" asked Lorraine. "That's what she wanted to do all the time. When we get back to Kendall Street, she'll be having the Carminellos or Mrs. Pulaski in to dinner."

"Oh, no, not quite that," said Georgia. "At least, not *all* the Carminellos. I wonder what Aunt Martha came to ask Mums."

Whatever it was, the two women were talking about it when the girls came back from taking the letter out to the mailbox.

"I hate to say no, Mart," Mrs. Lane said just as they came in. "But it doesn't seem as if I could do that."

"I'd make the shortcake, and have it all ready when you came home," offered Mrs. Allerton. "I'd love to do it."

"It isn't that," said Mrs. Lane. "It's just—oh, you know, Mart. I never meant to go into that house again."

Georgia looked hard at her mother. What house? And what was Aunt Martha asking Mums to do?

"Is it anything I could do for you, Mums?" she asked. "Lorrie and I have the whole afternoon we could use."

Aunt Martha shook her head and answered before Mrs. Lane had a chance. "I don't think anybody but Susie could do it, this time. I'm sure you girls couldn't."

Georgia looked anxiously from one to the other.

"Don't look like that, daughter. It isn't anything terrible, but I just would rather not."

Aunt Martha broke in again. "Mrs. Robinson, who opens Lane House to visitors every afternoon, is sick, and there's a very important group of people from a New York magazine coming to see it and maybe take some pictures. I hoped Susie would go up and show them the house. Nobody else knows enough about it to do it offhand."

"Oh," said Georgia. So that was it.

Mrs. Allerton rose and set the bowl of strawberries on the table. "Mine are all done," she said, "and when I've washed my hands I think I'll go out in the sunshine." Georgia felt sure she knew they would like to have her go.

"I hate to urge you, Susie," said Aunt Martha when Mrs. Allerton had gone, "but after all, you were happy there once."

"Happier than anywhere else in the world," said Mrs. Lane. "But you know how that was spoiled. I've come back to the town, and that hasn't been so bad as I thought it would be. But the house—"

"That might not be so bad either."

Georgia knew somehow that Mums would go. She would remember all that Aunt Martha had done to make living on Hackmatack comfortable for them. And she would know that a magazine article with pictures would be important to Aunt Martha and the other women who were trying to make Lane House support itself. And, maybe, like Georgia, Mums would want to see, at least once more, the house where they had been happy.

"It's like Mrs. Allerton," said Lorraine, suddenly, in her loud voice, and all three of the others looked at her, a little startled. Georgia was sure they had forgotten Lorrie was in the room.

"I mean," Lorraine went on, "she wouldn't unlock the door, but she was always unhappy because she didn't. And now she has—" there was an abrupt stop. "I guess it isn't anything for me to talk about. My dad always says I talk too much."

Mrs. Lane smiled, a rather thin little smile, but a smile nevertheless. "No harm done, Lorraine," she said. "Perhaps you are right. I'll give in, Mart. I'll unlock the door." And she went on hulling the berries in her bowl, even though her hands were not quite steady as she worked.

Aunt Martha's hand was not quite steady either, Georgia could see, as she reached over and laid it on Mrs. Lane's shoulder. But her tone was light as she said: "Thanks, Susie. Maybe someday you'll be glad it's unlocked. You're a good friend."

When Aunt Martha was leaving, she said, "I'll drive you up this afternoon, Susie, myself." And still in that light, easy way: "You might take the girls along. There's money to collect from people that might come in, you know, and the guest book to be signed. If they were there, it would leave you free for the great moguls. And besides, I know little George wants to see the room where she was born."

That was so Mums wouldn't be there alone to be sorrowful over the past. "We'd love to go," said Georgia quickly. "Let us, Mums!"

She was glad that her mother didn't know about Mona's latest thrust, and that Vee had kept them away long enough so that there was no trace of her burst of tears. Mums had her own battles to fight. She mustn't have to fight Georgia's as well.

It was nearly two o'clock when they stepped out of the car at the gate in the high white ornamental fence, with its delicate spindles, that enclosed Lane House.

"I won't come in, Susie," said Aunt Martha. "But I'll be back for you around five. The magazine people should be here soon, and I hope they won't stay every bit of the afternoon.

Here, little George, you're keeper of the keys," and she held them out in her hand. " 'By!"

Georgia went a step ahead to open the big front door.

"Oh," she said involuntarily, when they had stepped inside, "that must be the wing staircase!" and Lorraine echoed "The wing staircase!" going to stand at the broad foot and look first to the right and then the left from the point where it divided and wound gracefully up on the two sides.

"Is everything in the house grand like that?" Georgia asked. "I've been trying to remember."

"Of course not," said her mother. "It's just a house, and sometimes I used to think they put all their longing for grandeur into that one thing. That and the carvings."

"Where are they?" asked Lorraine.

"Everywhere. You can't miss them. Mantels, and the newel posts here at the staircase, and tiny little beaded moldings on the chair rails and around the paneling. The old story used to be that the first Lane, who had the house built, kept an English carver busy for three years here. I don't know if that's true, but it's what they said. The family was immensely proud of the carvings."

It was hard for Georgia to picture herself as living in Lane House and going up and down the handsome staircase. Struggling memories tried to break through, but it was easier to think of it as what it was now, a museum of earlier days. The rooms on either side the wide hall were large and high, and furnished like the ones they had glimpsed in Mrs. Allerton's house, with bygone elegance.

But before there was any chance to explore there were steps outside and Georgia flew to unlock the desk in the hall and lay out the guest book Aunt Martha had said she would find there. Mrs. Lane had disappeared somewhere, but came back now as the rather large delegation from the magazine came in. Georgia knew they were the magazine people, because there were camera men, and she was glad that Mums was there to receive them. She was sure she herself wouldn't know what to say. She looked at her mother, and could see that however much Mums had dreaded entering this house again, she was receiving the visitors as if she belonged just there, as indeed, Georgia remembered, she did.

There was a jumble of conversation. Reporters whipped out pencils and yellow pads, and Mrs. Lane was soon answering questions. The two girls sat back and caught what they could of information from the talk.

"How does it happen to be here, in this—this *hamlet?*"

"The Lanes in the beginning had a huge grant of land from the English king, and they made a fortune in that and succeeding generations, selling off great sections they did not need. By 1800, when this house was built, they could afford this kind of place. There are other houses of this sort, too, scattered along the coast and countryside."

"Who designed the staircase?"

"It is said to have been copied from a Bulfinch stair in a Boston mansion," Mrs. Lane replied.

And so on, question after question. Until, as Georgia had once said would happen, came: "What has become of the Lanes? How did the house come to be open like this to the public?"

Georgia listened for the answer and looked for any sign of suffering on her mother's face. There was none.

"The family has scattered and died out, as families do," she was saying. "So it was easy to give up the house to the public, as other such places have been given up. There are no Lanes left in Lane's Cove except us two," and she reached over to draw Georgia up beside her.

"We live in a smaller, homier place now. But I am Mrs. Lane, and this is my daughter Georgia, named for her father, the last George in a long line. My daughter was born in this house."

CHAPTER 18

"I, SUSAN BURNHAM . . ."

The girls waited impatiently for the visitors to go. Pictures were taken of the staircase, of the finest of the carved mantels, close-ups of paneling, and of beaded moldings. Then they began on room pictures.

"Better get them all," Georgia heard someone say. "Then we can pick the best ones." There was much scurrying back and forth, and, with it all, the endless questions.

"They'll have enough to make a book," said Lorraine.

"Probably they ask about everything, so they can pick and choose out of that too," Georgia answered. "They're coming down. They must be through."

"Glory be!" said Lorraine. "Bet your mother's glad. Gee! She does know all about it, doesn't she? They didn't stick her with a question once."

Georgia could see now what Aunt Martha meant by saying, "Nobody but Susie could do it," and she wondered how much of it all Mrs. Robinson could have told. She could hardly wait to see what the magazine would print, what the pictures would look like.

The whole delegation came trooping down the stairs, and

one young reporter, with his hat on the back of his head, stopped to say: "Too bad your mother wouldn't let us take your picture, too, Miss Lane, to go with the house. Staircases are all right, but I'm strong for the human side of the news, myself. Especially when—"

"Dempsey," someone at the front of the group called loudly, "we're leaving!" And Dempsey with a resigned shrug said, "Okay," then turned back to the girls with, "But I did want to finish that 'especially when.' It was going to be good."

"Thank you, Lorraine," Mrs. Lane said as she dropped rather wearily into a chair when they had gone. "You had the right idea. Unlocking the door was the thing to do."

"You were wonderful, Mums," said Georgia. "How did you ever get to know all that?"

"About the house? Oh, when your Grandfather Lane was living, he would talk about it by the hour, and you just had to listen. The house and the family were Gramp's hobbies, and he loved to talk."

"I want to see some of the things you talked about, myself. Come on, Lorrie, let's explore. Okay, Mums?"

"Yes. If I had any ambition left, I'd go with you. Your room, daughter, was the one on the sunny side, at the left of the staircase. Do you remember anything of the place, now you are here?"

"Vaguely, I think, and it's coming back," Georgia replied. "I still find myself expecting to smell the lilacs, even though lilacs faded weeks ago."

"The lilacs need to be pruned. They are like a forest. Someone ought to see to things like that. Now look around, and I'll just sit for a while. Another day we'll do it all together."

It was Vee who came to drive them back to the Point. "Ma

got held up," he said. "Some of those dear old friends from the city, that come in the summer. You know the kind. 'Only for a fifteen minute call,' they say and you're lucky if they aren't still there day after tomorrow."

Georgia locked the big door carefully when they were all out, and followed the others to the car. Suddenly she stopped. "Where was Annie?" she said. "I forgot all about her."

"In the back of the house," said Vee. "Don't you remember the side door? Annie's in where you saw her, knitting furiously, unless she has dropped asleep. That's where she always is, afternoons, when the house is open. Mornings, she dusts and sweeps and things like that."

"Which is the house she and Alice used to live in?" Georgia looked with interest across the narrow street.

"That old one, down by the big elm. Nobody's lived there since Annie went over to the Lane House." Vee pointed to a little gray house, not unlike the houses on the Point.

"Shouldn't think anybody would," said Lorraine. "The roof's fairly falling in."

"Yeah, whole house is falling apart. Have to come down before long. Neighbors don't like it there that way, spoils the street. But Annie won't sell, even if anybody would buy. Nothing to buy, pretty soon."

"Tell your mother, Vee," said Mrs. Lane when they reached the house, "that I'm glad I went. And if Mrs. Robinson isn't better and Mart needs me again, I'll do anything she asks."

"Better be careful, Susie," with one of those sudden loud laughs of his. "Ma might have some scheme up her sleeve."

That set Georgia to wondering, "What do you suppose that meant?" You never could tell, with Vee.

The shortcake was just out of the oven and the table set

when they reached the house. Mrs. Allerton had had a lovely time, Georgia was sure, and was as proud of the shortcake as if it had been the first one she had ever made. It was good, too, and the supper was gay.

"That's what Mrs. Allerton is really like," Georgia said afterward to Lorraine, as the two sat on the back doorstep watching the changing sky.

"Yes," said Lorraine. "I hope she won't have a relapse when we get back to Kendall Street."

"Oh, she can't," said Georgia. "She'll be having the Carminellos to dinner. You said so."

"Well, maybe. Sometimes I'm not so sure. That's a good deal to expect."

The sky was gorgeous now, pink and flaming gold, and they sat rather quiet till the colors had faded and the first star showed in the west.

"Same sky, same bright star, that we see at the foot of Cambridge Street," said Lorraine. "But everything else is different. It's so still. Honest, Georgia, don't you like it here?"

"I would," began Georgia slowly, "I really do, but—" She shifted the subject. "How do you like Vee?"

"Oh, he's all right, I guess. Kind of a noisy kid, though." Lorraine was definitely indifferent.

"I fought terribly with Vee when I first came," Georgia admitted, "but he just fought back and didn't hold any grudges. I think Vee's a pretty smooth product for a little town like Lane's Cove."

"He's a goon when it comes to railroads, though," said Lorraine. "Who does he think cares about how far it is to Oshkosh, or how long it takes to get to Chicago by some fancy train?"

Georgia sprang to Vee's defense. "He doesn't expect you to

be interested in those things just because he is. But I think it's pretty special to be interested, the way he is, in anything."

"I think you like the guy," said Lorraine.

"I think I'll notice the difference next year when he isn't here," Georgia answered soberly. "It's getting chilly. Let's go in."

They both turned their faces toward the doorway. "Listen, Lorrie," said Georgia. "We have company. I hear a man's voice."

"That wouldn't be Vee, would it?" Lorraine sounded amused.

"There are other men's voices besides Vee's," said Georgia. "And anyway, Mums would have called us."

The screen door sprang to with a sharp slap behind them as they entered the new little kitchen, brave with fresh paint and neatly stocked shelves and cupboards. Georgia looked out of its front window onto the driveway.

"There's a car," she said, "and not the Allens', either. Let's go in."

"Did you know," said Lorraine as they passed through the dining room, "that I gave up the interior decorating class after you went away? It wasn't any fun without you."

"No?" said Georgia. "Was that all you went for?"

"Mostly. I don't care too much about rooms and furniture and such like. And, besides, what chance do I have to do anything about it if I did like it? Nothing in our house ever gets changed. Now you—" and she paused expressively.

"It is one reason why I like it here," Georgia admitted. But they had reached the living room door and went in circumspectly to see who the caller or callers might be.

The Fairchilds! They really had come, and Mrs. Fairchild

greeted Georgia with: "Too bad Mona couldn't come with us. We waited till the school term was over so she'd have time, and now we picked the one night she couldn't make it. Somebody, I think she said Vee, was coming to take her to the movies. She said to tell you."

The Fairchilds proved to be pleasant people. He was dark and restless, ambling about the room, picking up a book here or a photograph there, and quick in his commendation of the changes they had made. She was small, like Mona, a faded blonde, full of conversation. Mona would be like her someday, beauty though Mona might be now.

Mrs. Allerton had gone to her own room, and the two girls sat in the background listening to the talk, Georgia wondering how much Mona's parents might know of Mona's enmity to George Lane's daughter.

When the callers rose to go, Mr. Fairchild said: "You went away so suddenly at the last, Susie, that we didn't even get to say good-by. And after that we lost track of you completely."

"Yes, Henry. That was my fault. I cut myself off from everybody here. I'm sorry. I had more friends than I realized then."

"I've never got over missing George around town," he said. "Takes a good man to be remembered that way. If it just hadn't been icy that day—" There seemed no way to finish that.

"We're glad you've come to live on Hackmatack," said his wife, "even if we've been slow to say so. You must come up to supper some night or to dinner Sunday, soon as Henry gets through haying. He's turned into a real farmer these days. You wouldn't believe it."

"Real farmer, yes and no," said Henry. "Raise our own beans

and potatoes, keep a cow, and have a garden, yes. But make our living entire that way, no, not by a jugful. Not with a kid that treats the mail order catalog like her own personal shopping list, with something coming parcel post about every other day."

But Georgia was sure he was proud of the kid and her purchases at that.

"Takes cash for mail order," he went on. "Not beans, nor potatoes. I make my living, Susie, and Henry Junior makes his, out of our two half-ton trucks. For a while we had the only dump trucks in town, and then we were busy. Now I've got competition, but I can charge double what I used to, and we're still busy. So Mona can have her gewgaws, and wife and I sit pretty comfortable too. Come, Hattie, thought we were going home. Come up, Georgia, see the kid. And bring your friend."

"Why, he's nice," said Georgia when she and Lorraine had begun to get ready for bed and were visiting back and forth through their open doors. "But did you get that about Mona? 'Somebody—I think it was Vee—' "

"Well, she had to have some excuse. I 'most wish she'd had to come. That would have been something. Do you suppose he did take her to the movies?" Lorraine appeared in her doorway, brushing the black hair vigorously.

"No, I don't. He said, she *used to be* a nice kid. You don't take anybody places for what she used to be."

"Oh, you might. Wait till I see him."

"Lorraine Fitzgerald! You wouldn't ask him?"

"Well, not if you're going to get all haired up about it." She laughed, not quite so loudly as she might have if it were not bedtime. "Don't know just what that means, unless it's your hair up on end. But I heard it, and I like the sound of it, anyway."

"Well, you lay off Vee," said Georgia emphatically. "And we'd better stop shouting back and forth, or Mums will be after us. G'night."

Next morning brought the first rainy day since Lorraine and Mrs. Allerton had arrived. "Come on, Lorrie," said Georgia, "let's prowl around in the attic. I love to hear rain on the roof, and there are heaps of things crowded in that little place that I want to look at. We might even find more clothes packed away in trunks or boxes."

"Maybe Azro's wife had a bonnet, too," said Lorraine. "Or somebody had a dress with a bustle. A real bustle, I mean, not just a bow or something on the back."

A few minutes later they were making their way into the attic as Georgia and her mother had done once before. "There's one thing in here that I'm going to have out," Georgia said as she worked her way along. "See, the little desk over in that corner. Do you think we could get it out over the tops of all these other things?"

"Maybe not over the top, but some way. Let's move a few of these small chairs and things out through the door into the porch chamber. That would leave a little space, and then we could get to the desk. It's worth trying." And she began promptly, lifting out a ladder-back chair with a broken leg, and then a child's velocipede, which she set down on the further side of the inner room.

"Look, Georgia," she called as she set the velocipede down. "Too bad you've got such long legs. This isn't even broken."

"Good! We can give it to the Allen kids. Take a hand on this table. It weighs a ton."

For the next half hour they pushed and pulled, stopping every now and then to admire or wonder at the taste of some earlier Burnham. But they were gradually getting to the desk, with some hope of getting it out.

"There!" said Lorraine. "Isn't it just as I said? Move the desk over here, then put the washstand in the space the desk came out of, and then—"

"Then drag every piece in the place to some other spot," laughed Georgia. "But I guess you're right. Look! That's a pretty thing, there on the old chest of drawers near the door. Jewel casket, might be, if anybody in a house like this had any jewels."

"Too big for that, and besides, I know what it is. It's a writing desk, to hold in your lap. My grandmother has one that she brought from Ireland with her when she first came. See!" and Lorraine reached over to open it up, while Georgia leaned to inspect the felt-lined interior, with its neat arrangement for paper, pens, and even a tiny square ink bottle set tightly into its own boxed space.

"See!" said Lorraine again. "This is the paper they used. Not so old-fashioned, either." She lifted the sheets.

"Maybe your Aunt Susan—" she stopped abruptly. Then, "Oh, Georgia, there's writing on this one. There's writing," she said again, looking up with a stricken face. "It says," and for once Lorraine's voice was not loud, " 'Last will and testament.' There, right in the middle of the page."

"Whose will?" said Georgia. "Whose, Lorrie? There must be a name."

Lorraine looked above those scary words in the middle of the page. " 'I, Susan Burnham,' " she read slowly. "Here, take it, Georgia. I don't know anything about wills."

"It says, 'Last will and testament.'"

"Neither do I, really," said Georgia, slowly. "I'd better take it down to Mums." Leaving everything where it stood, they headed for the stairs.

There were voices in the living room, and they burst in just in time to hear Aunt Martha say: "We'd want you to take charge of everything, Susie. Records, accounts, upkeep, publicity. Not just keeping the place open, the way Mrs. Robinson has. Everything. There isn't one of us has time, so things just don't get done."

She scarcely noticed the girls standing awkwardly in the doorway. And they, in their turn, knew that even a will must wait. What would Mrs. Lane say?

Aunt Martha went on: "She has wanted to give it up for a long time, but there wasn't anybody else, so she has stayed on. Now it's definite. Her son in Boston says she must come to them, and it's just providential that you're here. How about it?"

"I'd say yes in a minute, Mart, if I could be sure the old story wouldn't crop up and make trouble. Yesterday was all right. Those people were strangers. But I'm sure there'd be talk, and I'd hate to face it."

Aunt Martha was almost impatient. "Don't you know," she said, "how many friends you have? Everybody was so glad when Aunt Susan left you the house—"

This time Georgia did interrupt. "Mums," she said. "I don't think the house is ours. Herb was right. There is another will. 'I, Susan Burnham,' it says. Here," and she thrust the paper into her mother's hand. "Maybe we'll have to go away somewhere after all."

CHAPTER 19

WEDDING DRESS

"My soul and body," said Aunt Martha before the paper had more than changed hands, "what are you talking about, little George? There *isn't* any other will." And she reached out her hand in turn to take the paper from Mrs. Lane.

"And even if there were six," she went on, "they would all amount to the same thing. That was what Aunt Susan wanted to do. Half the fun she had those last years was planning for it. Laying up jars of food for Susie, wondering how Susie would fix the old house up, trying to feel sure the house would bring Susie back."

Georgia hoped Aunt Martha was right, but there was the will. "Last will and testament . . . I, Susan Burnham."

"What is this, then?" she asked.

Aunt Martha was turning the paper over and reading rapidly. Then she laughed. "Just one of those 'rough drafts' she used to make. She was so afraid Vince wouldn't get it exactly the way she wanted it. And she was always thinking of new things to do. This must have been the time she decided to give Herb $500, to keep him 'pacified,' so he wouldn't talk for the next ten years about breaking the will."

"It would take more than $500 to pacify Herb," said Mrs. Lane. "Then this really isn't anything? You had me scared for a minute, daughter."

"It isn't anything at all, Susie," said Aunt Martha. "See, it isn't even signed. Aunt Susan's will was her plaything. Ask Vince. He was very patient, changing it and adding to it, and then next time changing it back. But the main idea was always the same, give Susie the place. And the blueberry land on the barrens. What are you going to do about the berries? It's getting time to do something."

"I'd forgotten them, Mart. Are they worth much?"

"Worth plenty, in a good season," declared Aunt Martha. "Quick freezing's changed the whole blueberry business. That piece on the barrens might put little George through college, if you have good luck."

Aunt Martha turned to the two girls. "Go on back and play house in the attic, young ones, if you want to, but don't dig up anything else to scare Susie out of a year's growth. Never mind Herb. *There isn't any other will.*"

"I guess that's settled," said Lorraine as they went back, considerably subdued, to finish getting out the small desk.

"Yes," said Georgia, "and don't I feel silly. It wasn't even signed, and if we'd looked, it said as plain as day, give Herb $500. But what I'm really thinking about is Mums and the Lane House. 'I'd do it in a minute,' Mums said, 'if I could be sure the old story wouldn't crop up and make trouble.' Lorrie, if I only had that diary!"

"It might not tell you a single thing," said Lorraine. "What makes you think it would?"

"Alice knew something, or she wouldn't have worried about it all the time."

"Alice was sick, and growing sicker every day," said Lorraine. "She hadn't anything to do but worry. She felt bad about your father."

"And I feel bad about Mums, even if I did tell myself I was all through trying to find out anything. I'd better be, I know. Everybody's been swell to us, except Herb and Mona, and I don't really believe that many people feel about my father the way I thought they did. Okay! I'll give it up—again."

Georgia gave a big tug at the desk. "Here it comes." And a few minutes later, the desk was out and they had carried it triumphantly across the porch chamber and into Georgia's room.

"Now we'll go back and see if there's anything there for the show," said Georgia. "And if we see any papers, we won't even look at them. Is my face red?"

The second meeting of the Summer Club, at Mag's, brought a good deal of encouragement to the show committee, and enthusiasm in the members for Georgia's idea. They reported what, if anything, they had found at home, and some even brought things to be inspected and admired. The State Library had sent a book, *History of American Costume,* with pictures and descriptions of everything from Puritan caps and kerchiefs to hoop skirts and pantalettes.

"Now we can match dresses and dates, and get everything in order. We'll really have a lot of stuff," and Georgia set two members of the committee to work listing what the girls had to exhibit.

"I think there are things in the big attic at Lane House," said Edwina. "Ask your mother, George. She ought to know."

"I will, Eddie," said Georgia. "There might be things there."

Mums was still opening Lane House in the afternoons, and Georgia knew that before long the decision must be made about a permanent job there, taking on the whole management of the house, relieving the Historical Committee of all detail work. But Mums hated to decide.

"Are there any old clothes in the Lane House attic?" Georgia asked her mother that night, as they all sat in the dusk waiting for time to light the lamps. "Anything we could borrow for the show, I mean."

"Trunkfuls," Mrs. Lane answered. "And everything dated and ticketed. Gramp saw to that. It was almost as if he knew the house would be a museum someday. I wouldn't know about borrowing them, though. The Historical Committee would have to tell you about that."

"Could we go up to the attic and see the things?" asked Lorraine.

"Surely, but it would have to be when I could go up with you. Some of them must be pretty delicate by this time. The wedding dress and veil, for instance."

Georgia was all eager interest. "A whole wedding outfit? Could we borrow that?"

"You'd have to have a made-to-order model to wear the dress. That was a Burnham bride, Lucy Lorenzo's daughter, who married one of the George Lanes. She was Gramp's mother, and she was tiny. I've heard him tell."

"We'd have to find a tiny model then," said Georgia. "Mona!" she thought. "The half-pint kid." And before she knew it she had said it out loud.

"Yeah?" said Lorraine. "She wouldn't do it, even if you asked her. And you wouldn't ask her, even if you knew she'd do it."

"No," said Georgia. "I can't imagine asking her. But I'd love to show the dress. And the veil. Did anybody else ever wear that?"

"Yes. Other Burnham brides, and Lane brides, a whole list of them. I think I was the last one. If we hadn't let it go with the house, you might wear it yourself when you're a bride."

"You can borrow it," said Lorraine with a giggle. "You're a Lane, and belong to the house."

"I suppose I do. I was born there," Georgia admitted.

"I've been thinking," said Mrs. Allerton, who was so quiet most of the time that it was easy to forget she was there, "that you might make some very good scenes, tableaux, we used to call them, instead of just having your models come out and show off and go back one at a time. Grouping the costumes of one time together, of course."

"Wonderful! Magnificent!" said Georgia. "And then the announcer could talk about all of them, instead of flinging out a sentence now and another sentence five minutes later. Thank you, Mrs. Allerton. That's a real idea.

"It's going to take weeks, and weeks," she went on, "to get everything ready. See what I let myself in for."

"Oh, you can't fool me," Lorraine laughed. "You're having the time of your life. Only one thing you'd like better. Tearing a house to pieces, and putting it together some fancier way."

"She has good ideas about that, Lorraine, you'll have to admit. This is such a nice old room." Mrs. Allerton smiled before she went back to her reading.

The next few weeks flew by on wings. Someone suggested Currier and Ives prints for ideas, and told Georgia about a collection of them in a book lately published. That and more costume books came from the library at Augusta. One of the

Currier and Ives prints made Georgia remember the sleigh in the carriage house, and there was a hunt for ancient muffs and tippets. Liza sent word that she knew of a cradle that could be borrowed, if they really wanted to have a baby in the yard-long baby dress.

"It's like a snowball, rolling bigger and bigger every day," said Georgia.

She no longer had time to worry much about anything except the show, but when Mums told her one night that she had agreed to take entire charge of Lane House, Georgia's mind came back with a snap to the old bothersome questions.

"You're sure you want to?" she asked, sitting on her mother's bed before going to her own. "You won't mind what they say?"

"Not enough to keep me from doing it," Mrs. Lane replied serenely. "I need to earn something, and that's a job I can do, in a place where jobs aren't too easy to come by. Don't worry about me, daughter, and then I won't have to worry about you."

"You'll have to have a car," decided Georgia. "Vee can't trundle you about much longer. He'll be going away."

"That's being taken care of. We can have Mrs. Robinson's. Of course it's old, but if it wasn't, I couldn't pay for it."

"Will you have to be there all day every day?" asked Georgia.

"Sometimes. When they are pruning the lilacs, for instance. Or any other special thing I want to keep my eye on. But not all the time. Annie would think I was watching her too closely. I wouldn't want that."

"Will what they put in the magazine bring more people?"

"I'm sure it will," said her mother, "when it appears. But already there are more people, without it."

"Just from the road signs?"

"No, it seems that antiquarians and museum people are coming to know about the place. You should hear the experts argue, the way I have once or twice. One man wanted to have the whole interior torn out and set up in the American Wing in his museum."

"Honest? If they did that, you wouldn't have a job after all."

"They won't. But all the talk brings more people, and people are what will pay me for managing the place."

"I am glad the Historical Committee said we could use the costumes from the attic," said Georgia. "Especially the wedding dress. That fits right into the Civil War time. Special wedding scene, with the groom and other men in blue uniforms, and all those wonderful hoop-skirt dresses for the girls. We have more of those than anything else. They are so beautiful people wouldn't throw them away, I guess."

Sometimes, though, Georgia wondered whether they would be able to use the wedding dress after all. There were strings attached to the permission. No squeezing someone into it that it really didn't fit. The dress was old now, and old satin had a way of going all to pieces under strain.

One of the girls had suggested that they find a twelve-year-old, or even a tall ten-year-old to wear it.

"Oh, *no!*" chorused the rest of the committee. "A bride with a baby face?" And, "Besides, at that age they haven't any *shape*. Their stomachs stick out."

And Mag clinched the matter with: "It's Mona, or no wedding dress. Take it or leave it, George."

"Okay, then, I'll take it. But somebody else will have to ask her. I won't. And I haven't any idea she'll do it, anyway. She'd love to say no, just because I thought up the idea."

"Poo-ooh! Pass up a chance to be the center of the best scene we've got? You don't know Mona."

"I know her enough," said Georgia. "She'll make a good-looking bride," grudgingly. "I suppose that's all I need care about. The audience can't see inside her."

It was fine that the stage entrance to the Town Hall was wide enough to admit the old sleigh, and the girls had all worked hard to paste a thin layer of cotton wadding to big sheets of paper for snow. The main trouble with that scene was the horse. There must be one, but what horse, even if you could get him on the stage, would leave the "snow" intact even for a minute under his feet?

"He ought to be a wooden one, that would keep his feet still," said Lorraine.

"Well," said Myrt Pinkham, popping up from her chair in the corner, "I know where there's one of those, but he's a long way off, in Machias."

"An honest-to-goodness horse, not a hobbyhorse, or a rocking horse?" Everybody clamored at once.

"It's a horse, all right. He used to stand out in front of my grandfather's shop. I've heard them say he cost a lot of money, but they sold lots of horses and harness in those days. They could afford to splurge. People came from all over Washington County to Pinkham's Sales Stable and Harness Shop. Big business!" Myrt was enjoying her moment in the limelight.

"Machias isn't a long way off, these days," said Mag. "He can come over in a truck."

"I hope horsie doesn't look wooden," said Georgia. "If he doesn't, he's an answer to prayer."

"Oh, he's a spirited animal, all right," said Myrt. "I used to climb on his back and pretend I was Paul Revere."

One by one, the scenes shaped up. Every girl in the Club but Georgia had a costume to model and a part to play, some of them two or three. But Georgia refused to be on the stage at all.

"My job is in back," she said over and over in answer to demands that she wear this or that. "There's plenty of work, making the performance go without any hitches, and that's what I intend to do. A few of the boys will help, if somebody tells them what needs to be done. I'm going to be that somebody. I told you long ago that I haven't any platform talents, but I'm not too bad backstage."

Mrs. Lane's having the car was a help in getting places. Georgia wished that she might learn to drive, but there was little time for anything except the business of the show. Club meeting once a week was a relaxation. One meeting took the form of a picnic at Fountain Rocks, and another a whole day among the islands from Petit Manan to Roque. Two fathers gave their motorboats and their services that day and the boys were invited.

"This will be something to remember when I get holed up for the winter up back country," said Vee. They were standing on the highest spot of one of the outermost islands, looking out to sea. "Nothing between us and Europe, if we could just see across."

"You've been here before," said Georgia.

"Been coming all my life. But you're in luck today. Can't always land on Jordan's Delight. Never can on the sea side."

The sea, almost black in the sunlight, rolled in great rounded swells at the foot of the high clifflike head, and Georgia was reluctant to turn back.

Curt was rowing the skiff in which she was ferried back to

the motorboat. "Hi," Curt had said, briefly, as Vee had helped her on board, and Georgia remembered the last time she had seen Curt, and his "Let me think." Was he still thinking, she wondered, or had he forgotten the whole matter long ago?

He rowed along now as if he were alone in the boat, except for an occasional, "Keep her trimmed, there," when somebody leaned too far to one side, and "Watch your step," as he handed them up one by one to the higher level of the motorboat deck.

When Georgia came, last, to be helped, she said, "Give me a boost, Curt. Looks a long step up."

"Yeah," he said. Then in the instant he was lifting her, he added, "I been thinking, as I said."

Georgia leaned down from above to say, "Thank you," and Curt spoke again. "Not much to show for it, but I haven't forgot. May be a way yet."

"Just the same thing our fathers and mothers used to do," said Vee, on the way home, "but it's one thing that's still fun."

"Ancestors' fashions," called Edwina from up ahead. "How about it, chairman? Have a scene in the show?"

"It's the first time today that I've thought of the show," said Georgia, surprised. "The first time I've thought of anything except what a swell time I was having."

No, there was once, she remembered, thinking of Curt. *"I haven't forgot, though. Maybe I'll find a way yet."* Of course he couldn't, but it was nice of him to try. She had really, she reminded herself, given up trying to solve the mystery. She mustn't even think of it any more.

CHAPTER 20

UNDER THE ROOF

"They aren't tearing the Soames house down after all," said Mrs. Lane one night at the supper table. "A whole gang of men was there today, putting on a new roof. Everybody in the neighborhood will be glad."

"Does Annie still own it?" asked Georgia. "I thought she hadn't any money to fix it."

"She must have sold it. Herb was there working, and I'm sure he would be delighted to tell me all about it if I wanted to ask. I think he might be in charge of the job. The others were mostly youngsters. Vacation jobs, probably. It's hard to get men in blueberry time."

"Hard to get boys, or even girls," said Georgia, "from what I hear. Almost everybody I know is going to rake, or raking already."

"Raking?" Mrs. Allerton looked astonished. "Blueberries?"

"Well, not with a regular rake. It's a special kind, to get a lot of berries at a time. I saw one Marion had. She was going to start raking the next day. Going to earn all her fall clothes, she said. Maybe I ought to be earning my fall clothes, too."

"I'd say you have your hands full without that," said Lorraine. "If you raked berries all day, you'd be sleepier than the others are, come night and rehearsals."

Rehearsals were really becoming difficult to arrange, with so many of the cast "dog tired," as Vee put it, when night came. But the picking season was fairly short, and the date of the show had been put almost at the end of August.

"When it's over, I have to go home," said Lorraine.

"Have you had a good time?" asked Georgia bluntly.

"I wish I'd just come, and it was all ahead of me. I couldn't say more than that, could I?"

"I'll say the same," said Mrs. Allerton. "And I must go home then, too. I have some plans for this fall, and the winter. New plans. I wouldn't have missed this, and I hope you'll let me come back next year."

"Me, too. There'll be Summer Club again."

"And somebody else can be chairman of the show committee," said Georgia. "I'll have earned the right to be just one of the crowd."

"That's so. But it isn't next year yet, and there's rehearsal at seven-thirty. Vee'll be here in no time now, to get us."

"Seems like schooltime, Vee coming, and then stopping to get Sour Puss in the front seat." Georgia made a derisive face.

"*Who* is Sour Puss?" asked Mrs. Allerton.

"Mona," explained Lorraine. "She has one of those cases of 'I don't speak to you.'"

"Never mind," said Georgia. "She jumped at the chance to be bride, when Mag asked her, just as Mag said she would. I bet she feels like the cat with the canary tucked away inside her. We've let her have Vee for the groom, haven't we?"

"Sure have. What more could she ask?" laughed Lorraine.

"Well, she might like it if he were more enthusiastic. Vee's definitely off Mona these days. Guess he thinks she's catty, with or without the canary."

"She shouldn't be catty, then," said Lorraine. "It's her own fault."

It was Lorraine who had the idea of using not only the sleigh from the carriage house, but also the surrey for a summer scene. *Summer Afternoon,* they decided to call it, and they had the date somewhere around 1913, in the hobble-skirt era.

"That will make it fine," she said. "Have someone getting in when the curtain goes up, and having to pull her long tight skirt over her knee so she can get her foot on the step."

There were still plenty of horses and carryalls even as late as 1913. Only a few people had automobiles. Of course they would have to use the same wooden horse, but after all a horse was a horse, and that wouldn't matter.

Vee came to help them get the sleigh and the carryall out.

"Why not use the buggy too?" he said. "Fellow takes his girl for a ride. Or do it with a real horse, not at the show, but drive around town in the daytime, to advertise the show. Have them in fancy clothes, all rigged up. Fix the horse up with one of those nets they used to have to keep the flies off—"

"And have the girl carry that tiny carriage parasol that Marion brought in. I've been wondering what to do with it. Vee, you're a genius." Georgia beamed.

"Just found that out?" said Vee modestly. "Thought you knew it from the first. I'll make a martyr of myself and borrow Curt's colt, Hurricane, and I'll drive him up and down Main Street, little George, if you'll be the girl."

"Me?" said Georgia.

"Yes, you. Nobody thinks it's fair for you to get out of wearing any funny old clothes at all. And that's one time you can't crawl out with any talk of being needed backstage. Fellow takes his girl to the County Fair. How's that?"

"Maybe Curt would rather drive Hurricane himself," protested Georgia.

"Curt? Huh, you know he couldn't be hired to do it. Bet you had plenty argument to get him to be the father in the wedding scene."

"We certainly did. It was Lorrie finally persuaded him. I don't know how, but she did."

"He's good, though," said Vee, "in the Prince Albert coat, and carrying the plug hat. No, you'll have to put up with me for the buggy ride. And you'll have to do it. I'll get your whole committee to shout you down if you dare refuse. Okay. Fellow takes his girl to the County Fair." And he went, whistling, into the depths of the carriage house to drag the buggy out before Georgia could possibly say no.

At rehearsal that night, the wedding scene was to be put on. When they stopped at the Fairchilds' on the way to the hall, Mona surprised Georgia with, "Hi, girls," as she took her place on the front seat beside Vee.

The two in the back seat looked at each other with raised eyebrows, and Lorraine muttered: "Getting too many cold shoulders nowadays. Probably wishes she hadn't acted like a goon."

This was dress rehearsal for the wedding scene, and they waited impatiently for Curt, who was very late.

"What is he, raking?" asked Georgia.

"No, hasn't raked at all this year," said Edwina. "Been working at the Soames house. His father bought it."

Georgia wished that Curt had told her. There might have been some chance that she could look around there before they began work. But she had little time to spend in regret. Curt came in, and hurried off to a dressing room to put on the black suit with the long coat and come back with the old beaver hat in his hand. The rehearsal went into action.

"This scene," began the announcer, "shows a wedding in Lane's Cove in 1863. The bridal gown and veil were really worn by Lucetta Burnham, who married George Lane (one of the earlier George Lanes) home on furlough from the Union Army in that year. The groom and several of the guests are in authentic uniforms of the period—"

Mona did look beautiful in the yellowed old satin, with the lace veil rippling out over the long train. And Vee made a good-looking groom in the old army blue. The mother, in pencil-striped silver gray with enormous hoop skirt, and Curt stiffly dignified beside her, were authentic to the period too. The guests were largely feminine, in the same widely extended skirts, though there was a sprinkling of uniforms and black-coated older men.

"That's our masterpiece," Georgia said with a sigh, "and I wouldn't have believed we could do it. It's lucky we could rent hoop skirts from that costume company in Boston. People must have saved the dresses and thrown the hoop skirts away."

"They rusted. After all, it's a long time since hoop skirts went out."

"That's right. Now, everybody. Be on hand early Tuesday night. Take your costumes home with you, because there's no safe place here to keep them. But handle them carefully. You know about that. This is the scene that's going to stop the show. I think it's perfect, even if it is just a kids' show. That's all."

There was a general rush for dressing rooms. The stage cleared as if by magic, and Georgia stood up from her seat in the sixth row, reaching mechanically behind her for her coat. Lorraine was deep in conversation with Eddie, out in front, and Vee had already gone to bring the car to the door. Georgia started forward to join Lorraine, but Curt stopped her, holding out a small package.

"Did find a way," he said. "Persuaded Pop the Soames house was a good buy, to fix up and sell again. And it is," he added parenthetically. "We're working on it now. Gave me a good chance to look around. Search, you might say, and today I found what you wanted." Thrusting the package into Georgia's hand, he retreated quickly. "Be seeing you," he said. "Be kind of careful of it. But I guess you will, anyway." And Curt was gone.

"Curt," Georgia called a little wildly. "Curt!"

But he had disappeared, and Vee, coming in, said, "Want me to get him?"

"No," said Georgia, "I'll see him tomorrow."

Clutching the package tightly, all the way home she was thinking, "Will it tell me anything? It must, or Curt would not have said, 'Be careful!'"

The way home seemed longer than it had ever seemed before, and she scarcely heard the conversation going on around her. Perhaps she did realize that there was more conversation than there had been lately when Mona was with them, but it made no impression on her. In her hands was the diary. Nothing else mattered.

She made up her mind that she would not tell Mums until she had read it by herself, and had found out whether it told anything new. She tried to make her good night to Vee easy and natural, and when she was in the living room, to answer questions about the rehearsal and to listen patiently while Lorraine told what a spectacular success the wedding scene was going to be.

"Honestly, I can't wait for Tuesday night," Lorraine said. And Georgia thought, "And I can't wait for tonight, upstairs, when the rest of you aren't there."

"What's the matter with you, dopey?" Lorraine said cheerfully, when they finally started to go to their rooms. "You've been in a daze ever since we left the hall. Did the wedding scene go to your head?"

"Could be," said Georgia. She lighted the kerosene lamp on her bureau, and snapped off the flashlight that had lighted her upstairs. "But I guess I can sleep it off. Good night."

No talking things over tonight. She couldn't stand it. "I have to know," she whispered to herself. "I'll make it right with Lorrie tomorrow." Abruptly, she closed her door.

CHAPTER 21

HOME AT LAST

Coming close to the light, she laid on the bureau the stout manila envelope Curt had given her. For a second, dreading possible disappointment, she stood looking at the imprint, "Kennedy Stock Farm," in an upper corner. But Curt had said, "What you wanted," and for safekeeping he had sealed it tightly here.

With hands that were fumbling and unsure, she tore the envelope open.

Inside she found a paper-covered notebook that said "Composition" on its side, and inside its few penciled pages, another, smaller envelope sealed in its turn. Georgia wondered what it contained, but she laid it aside. She would read what Alice had written, first.

She began to read:

"I never meant to write any more about it," the story began. "I stopped my diary so I should not be tempted to put it there. It didn't come out the way I thought it would, the way I meant it to. I might have known it wouldn't. And now there isn't any way I can make it right.

"The doctor I saw in Portland said maybe six months. It is almost that now. Liza has been here taking care of me for a long time, and it won't be long before I won't be able to get out of bed at all. So if I do anything, it will have to be soon. That is why I am writing this now.

"None of it would have happened if it hadn't been icy that day. When George's car ran off the bridge and everybody was running down there, saying he was dead, something put it into my head, and I took the money out of his desk. The tide was high, and I thought I could make them think the money was lost in the water.

"I meant to use it to buy some kind of annuity for Annie, so she would be safe after I was gone. Annie couldn't take care of herself. I thought I could do it, or perhaps I didn't really think at all. I wish now I had.

"What I did with the money then doesn't matter now. They didn't find it and I brought it home. But I didn't know how to do anything with it after I got it. I had changed one of the big bills into small ones there before anyone came back to the bank, and I have used that much of the money to pay Liza. I didn't want Annie to have a debt hanging over her. But what I wanted to do for my sister I didn't dare even to try.

"The rest of the money I still have. And I am hiding it with this. Someday they will find it, but I won't be here, and maybe Annie won't either. I think I've got a place to hide it that they won't find very easily. It may be a long time.

"I worry about Annie, and I am sorry about Susie and little George. If I had more courage I would tell the whole thing now, but I don't seem to have any courage at all. I do hope they find this sometime, and clear George. I didn't mean to have them think he did it. He was a good man."

"Mums! Mums!" Georgia cried. "Mums, I can't wait for tomorrow!" And she plunged through the doorway into her mother's darkened room.

"Curt did it," she said in wild excitement. "I mean Curt found it, and it was Alice all the time. Alice, Mums! And even the money's here." She had cast herself on her mother's bed, and went babbling on in the dark.

"Georgia, Georgia," said her mother. "Wait a minute, get your breath and let me get mine. I think I'd better light the lamp."

And while she scratched the match and brought its flame to the little bedside lamp, Georgia waited, hugging herself in the chilly night air and wondering if what she had read could really be true. But it had to be. She had the money right there, in her own hands.

"Now," said her mother. "Begin at the beginning."

"Read it," said Georgia, thrusting the book toward her mother. "Read it. I can't really believe it yet."

Holding the penciled pages close to the small flame of the lamp, Mrs. Lane sat there on the side of the bed in her nightgown and read, while Georgia tried to wait quietly for her to finish.

At last Mrs. Lane laid the book down. "Poor Alice," she said. "But it proves that all of us who had faith in George were right. He *couldn't* have done a thing like that."

Georgia look at her mother. "You aren't excited a bit," she said.

Mrs. Lane smiled. "Yes," she said slowly, "I'm excited. New

England fashion, maybe. But I'm glad of one thing. We came back before we knew. That way we've found how good people really are."

"If we hadn't come back, we wouldn't know. Curt hunted for the book because I asked him to. I mean I told him how I wished I could find it—"

"Where was it?" asked Mrs. Lane.

"I don't know. Curt said, 'Here's what you wanted,' and pushed it into my hand and rushed off. Sometimes I'd like to shake that boy."

Then there was the money to be looked at and wondered about.

"Poor Alice," said Mrs. Lane again. "Her last days spoiled, and all for nothing. It would have been better, as she says, if she had taken time to think."

"Mums, you're cold," said Georgia as her mother shivered a little. "Get back into bed. I'll go and get undressed, and then would you mind—your bed's good and big—if I came back and got in with you? I don't think I could be happy enough there all by myself."

"Yes, come back. And there are all the days ahead to be happy in."

Georgia scurried into her own room, pulling off clothes as she went.

Next day there was Lorraine to tell, and Mrs. Allerton, whom they had tried to keep in the dark about the whole thing.

"I knew something was wrong," she said. "And now it has righted itself, the way things sometimes do. Not that I under-value what the boy did," she added hastily, "nor what you did, Georgia, to get him into action. That's an achievement, in itself."

The money and notebook, Curt told them that day, had been pushed into the center of a tight bundle of shingles in the attic, shingles left over probably from mending the roof years before. By pulling out two or three in the middle of the bundle there had been room to thrust the book and money in out of sight.

"And I'd never have noticed them if I hadn't been hunting," he said. "We had plenty shingles we brought for the new roof, and nobody saw those few in the attic. But I was practically using a microscope on the place, so I hauled the bundle out under the skylight. There was something in it. I could see something. 'That's the baby,' I said. Had to be. School composition books don't belong in amongst shingles. Lucky somebody was hunting."

Was there anything left to wish for? It seemed to Georgia that there was not. "Nothing can hurt Alice any more," her mother had consoled her when she found it hard to forget Alice's unhappy story. "And nobody would be heartless enough to tell Annie. She doesn't see many people, and those she does see wouldn't want to hurt her like that. Nobody needs to tell her anything."

The written story and the money went first to Uncle Vince, and then to the bank officials.

"The money you left with us ten years ago," a letter from the bank to Mrs. Lane said in reply, "was duly credited to an account we opened for you, then. It is there, subject to your order now. We have used it, as we use all deposits, and it has accumulated interest, as deposits do. We are glad, too, that your husband's memory can no longer be questioned by any kind of gossip. And we are glad that we found nothing then to lead us into questioning it. We always believed in George Lane."

Then it was Tuesday, one of those bright blue days that have the, feel of autumn in the air. Georgia was ready when Vee appeared, driving Hurricane harnessed to the buggy. Ready for what the committee called "the circus parade," to advertise and remind the public that tonight *Ancestors' Fashions* would be presented by the Summer Club at the Town Hall.

"Gee! Some get-up," said Vee, and sang, *Where did you get that hat?* "I don't see what you need of the parasol with that cartwheel on your head."

"Frills and furbelows is what I call this whole outfit," said Georgia, "and I feel as if I had on three or four pairs of ruffled bedroom curtains."

"Well, it must have been the style. And what about me? Don't overlook my la-di-da outfit. All I lack is a handle-bar mustache."

"You're a wow without it," said Georgia. "I love the little derby hat, and if clothes were ever made of a larger plaid than that, I'd like to see them. Don't ever tell anybody that that suit came from the costume company. Nobody's attic had anything half loud enough to advertise *Ancestors' Fashions*. And no announcer has to say anything about us. We're strictly on our own. Here's the placard."

Vee tied it conspicuously on the back of the buggy, and helped Georgia ceremoniously to the left side of the high seat. She raised the tiny carriage parasol and he, clucking "Giddap" to Hurricane, waved the whip gaily to Mrs. Allerton and Lorraine, who stood by to see them off.

"Don't let that whip touch him," said Georgia nervously. "I don't think he'd like it. And I'm sure he doesn't like that net thing with the tassels, hanging over his back."

"Ah," said Vee, "I see you don't get asked out for a buggy ride very often, my girl."

"I surely don't," said Georgia. "And I hope you know how to drive a horse."

The "circus parade" was a great success, Georgia was sure, if laughs and shouted salutations were any indication. They went everywhere, stopped before Lane House, the stores and the post office, and at any number of individual homes, where Vee's loud "Whoa!" was all that was needed to bring people to their doors.

When the town clock struck the half hour after four, Georgia said: "Now take me home. If we don't have an audience it won't be our fault. And I've got to rest up a little for tonight."

"You'll have an audience, my girl," declared Vee. "And I bet they'll say this is the best show the Summer Club has ever had."

"I wish they might. But I don't care the way I did. Making an impression on Lane's Cove doesn't seem so important as it did. But I hope we make a lot of money. The school can use it."

"I'll say," agreed Vee.

It seemed no time at all to Georgia after she got home before the evening was there, the hall was crowded, the show was on, and then was ended. People did say it was the best the club had given. Nobody seemed to want to go home, and people clamored around the show committee to offer congratulations and to meet the chairman, "George Lane's kid."

"I knew your father," most of the older ones began. And, "Where's your mother? I must be sure to see her." The story of the notebook and who had been responsible for the loss of the bank money was being whispered everywhere, Georgia knew.

But nobody said anything directly to her until Uncle Vince

came, saying: "You did it after all. I shouldn't have given up the way I did. But I don't mind saying now that everything I did find out seemed to point to George. And he was my friend, dead and unable to defend himself."

"That's why you tried to warn me off," said Georgia.

"Yes. I thought we, any of us, would do better just to let people forget. I never believed he did it, but I couldn't prove it."

"Didn't anybody ever suspect Alice?" asked Georgia.

"I don't think so," Uncle Vince replied. "She seemed such a timid soul. But she wasn't so simple as we thought."

"I didn't really do a thing, you know," said Georgia, "except to stir up other people. Or try to. It was Curt who did it, and all we can do in return is to say a sort of thin 'Thank you.'"

"He isn't looking for thanks," said Uncle Vince. "He knows how you feel."

Then Herb and Liza came up, and Liza tried to tell Georgia how good the show had been. But Herb couldn't wait to put in his word.

"Glad to see you're doing something besides tearing the house to pieces," he began. "But I s'pose you'll be back at it again. What you going to rip out next?"

"Let the house rest, Herb," said Liza, but he wouldn't be stopped. "Hear Suze has got money in the bank," he said. "You can do a lot with that—to my house."

Liza laughed her lazy, comfortable laugh. "Don't know what Herb would do," she said to Georgia, "if he didn't have something to jaw about. 'Twasn't the house, 'twould be something else. But don't you mind. He'll be off on another tack before long. That will has lasted him a long while." They went off into the crowd and Georgia wondered again how Liza stood it to have Herb around all the time.

After that Tuesday night the days flew until Lorraine and Mrs. Allerton were leaving. The house seemed empty and quiet when they were gone, especially when Mrs. Lane had to be at Lane House.

"You don't really have to do it now, Mums," Georgia said one day when her mother came home tired in the late dusky afternoon.

"I think I do need to. In a week or two now you will be in school all day, and I'd be the one alone here. Lane House will be my way of making contact with people, the way school is for you. And when you go away next year I'll have something to keep me busy. And out of mischief," with a little laugh.

"Everything is different now, isn't it, Mums?"

"Yes," said her mother, "it is. When we came, it was really as I said, just the surety of a roof over our heads, in a time when I couldn't see ahead very far. Now everything *is* different. And I don't mean just money in the bank, and a job."

"The money is good, though," Georgia told her. "We can do more things to the house, and—could we look out for Annie, by and by, if she needs it? She hasn't anybody at all."

Mrs. Lane nodded. "I'm planning for that. The money she got for her house will last for quite a while. After that, we'll see that she is all right. What Alice did I thought had spoiled my life, and the life I could make for you. But my life wasn't spoiled, and yours—"

"Will be what I make it—I hope. You told me that once and I thought you were hardhearted. Maybe not, though. I'm not sure I'll be much good at making a life, but I don't mind trying."

A few weeks later, it was Vee who was going away. "See you Thanksgiving," he said when he came to say good-by. "When

I get some standing in this institution I'm going to, I'll ask you to come to that Winter Carnival we've all heard so much about. Maybe next year. By that time you'll be in an institution too and if I'm good you might ask me to a prom."

They were at the door now, and Vee turned back to say, "Aunt Susan did a good job bringing you here, and if I have good luck—"

He broke off with, not the loud laugh, but the smile, wide as always. "S'pose we might leave that for unfinished business. So long, little George."

Georgia watched him back the car out to the road. It was good to know that he would be coming home for Thanksgiving. She picked up Pom, who was making little crooning noises at her feet, and turned back to the house that was no longer only a roof.

Wisconsin State College at Eau Claire
LIBRARY RULES

No book should be taken from the library until it has been properly charged by the librarian.

Books may be kept one week but are not to be renewed without special permission of the librarian.

A fine of two cents a day will be charged for books kept over time.

In case of loss or injury the person borrowing this book will be held responsible for a part or the whole of the value of a new book.

DUE	DUE	DUE	DUE
Mar 10 '58	Oct 27 '60		
Mar 31 '58	Nov 7 '60		
Sep 16 '58			
Sep 23 '58	Mar 1 '61		
Oct 9 '58	Mar 13 '61		
Nov 6 '58			
Nov 20 '58	May 26 '61		
Dec 11 '58	Jan 15		
Feb 27 '59	Apr 23		
Mar 9 '59	Sep 16 63		
Mar 26 '59			
May 8 '59	31 '63		
Jul 13 '59	4		
May 31 '60			
Sep 29 '60			